POWER
IN TIME

POWER IN TIME

A Kynaston Royal Saga

Epoch 1

BY
ERUDESSA GENTIAN

ISBN Paperback: 978-1-7352075-1-3
ISBN Electronic: 978-1-7352075-2-0

Library of Congress Control Number: 2020913635

Portions of this book are works of fiction. Any references to historical events, real people, or real places are used fictitiously. Other names, characters, places and events are products of the author's imagination, and any resemblance to actual events or places or persons, living or dead, is entirely coincidental.

Printed in the United States of America.

Erudessa Gentian
Address

www.ErudessaGentian.com

POWER IN TIME

Prologue

Dual-tinted gaze of one just and fair
With import and power beyond compare
Family bonds bring steadfast strength
Faithful and loyal to whatever length
But a strength can always be turned around
And what is lost will not always be found

— From Evren's Foundation Prophecies

CHAPTER 1

The poisoned, old gentleman stumbled into the dark, stinky alley. He had forgotten how dirty Earth's cities in the early twenty-first century could be. No one was passing by the alley's entrance yet, but he pulled his hat low over his eyes, tightened the long black coat that materialized around him, and started making his way toward the early morning light streaming in from the street. With each step, the small bag slung over his shoulder lightly tapped against his thigh.

He had to find her before it was too late. He owed her that much. It was his fault she was in this mess. Well, mostly his fault. But now, he was her only hope—as long as he could get them to her. He didn't have time to invent anything else.

Pausing at the alley's entrance, he stopped against a wall and clutched his chest. Poisons could burn like nothing else. He had to wait for the pain near his heart to subside before he could continue on his quest.

I have to find her.

That was his all-consuming thought. To give her his one last gift. It would protect her. Help her reach the full potential she didn't even realize she had.

Hope surged in him as he heard a young, lilting voice down the street. Carefully stepping around insect-infested piles of trash bags, he peeked out of the alley to make sure of the voice's owner. It took years for him to get this close. But just as he caught sight of the young woman he was dying for, his view was blocked by a stained black t-shirt with a white skull and crossbones decorating the chest of a man who pushed him back into the shadowed alley. Another man followed behind skull and crossbones.

"Hey, old man." The larger thug pinned him against the grimy wall with a sweaty, shaky, but surprisingly strong arm. "Hand over your wallet, phone, everything. Wouldn't want to hurt you."

The trapped man let out a gasp as the deceptively small, poisoned cut below his left collarbone tore open a bit more. He ignored the trickle of blood that steadily began soaking his clothing as he observed the two thieves.

They both sported tattoos on nearly every inch of exposed flesh. The smaller one was practically skin and bones, with bloodshot eyes and bruises all along his arms from obvious needle pricks. He also brandished a knife and, the scientist thought, looked like he did too want to hurt him.

ϟϟϟ

Larkspur Bei stepped out of the used bookstore, a bag bulging with biology textbooks swinging on her arm and an equally full backpack hanging from her shoulders. As Lark strode down the sidewalk, noisy evidence of a scuffle from an alley across the street broke into her tranquil thoughts of where to get a study snack.

Lark tried to ignore it.

Don't get involved.

She gripped the straps of her backpack with tight fingers, resisting the urge to massage her neck.

You've helped enough people around here. You're leaving today. On to a new chapter.

"You'll only regret it," she muttered to herself, even as she carefully tucked her sunglasses away.

She touched a pair of dog tags tucked safely under her shirt, then started jogging toward the dark alley.

More grunts, then, "Now you're going to get it, old man!"

Lark broke into a run.

ϟϟϟ

"I don't have anything useful to you," the old gentleman told the thieves truthfully.

His back was still pressed against the rough, dirty brick of a surrounding building. He could feel the uneven edges through his coat.

"You'd be surprised how inventive people can be," the knife holder spat. "Cough it up. Everything you've got."

The scientist struck out with much more speed and force than his attackers expected. The larger thug stumbled back from a punch to the throat, eyes glazing in pain. The smaller one nearly blacked out thanks to a steel-toe boot finding its way to his groin. Dropping his knife, the unfortunate thief fell to the trash-strewn pavement with a gasp.

It was too much for the bleeding man. He cried out as he crumpled to the ground, hat falling off his head. His chest felt like it was being ripped open with flames. The poison was working quicker now. He could actually feel himself dying.

The bigger of the two thieves recovered enough to growl angrily. "Now you're going to get it, old man!"

He looked up to see the thug pull a gun from behind his back.

Then suddenly, he didn't have it.

A dark-haired young woman dropped a bag on the ground at the alley's entrance, thick books spilling out onto the sidewalk. Blindsiding the aggressor, she managed to kick the gun out of his grasp. She smoothly sidestepped the thug's clumsy attempt at a hook. When the man almost fell forward, the woman took advantage of his partially exposed back, smashed a downward elbow into the back of his neck, causing him to stumble down on one knee. His dazed eyes didn't even see her round kick to his jaw, knocking him into unconsciousness.

The smaller attacker crawled away in the scuffle, a putrid pile of vomit the only evidence left of him. The woman grabbed a pair of latex gloves from her backpack, slipped them on and pressed her fingers to the throat of the thief she knocked out. Her shoulders relaxed with a relieved sigh. Using the attacker's own belt, she bound his arms behind him before stepping lightly to the pistol. She checked the chamber to see if it was loaded, then fiddled with a little lever on the side before tucking it into her backpack.

The young woman kneeled next to the injured man "Sir? Are you all right? My name is Lark. I'll—" She paused mid-sentence, finally getting a good look at him. "F-Franklin?"

"Finally," he whispered, laying an affectionate hand on her cheek. He looked up into the face he had been searching so hard for. There was the mesmerizing combination of blue right eye and gray left eye, both now wide with shock.

"Dr. Franklin Wright? Is it really you?" She squinted at him. "What happened to your hair?"

He had been clean-shaven with his hair dyed white the last time they met. The aquamarine of his natural hair interspersed with silver threads would be unnatural for this era.

"What am I thinking?" Lark berated herself. "Are you hurt?"

"Merely had the wind knocked out of me," he lied with a wince as she helped prop him against the wall. "Just give me a moment." He didn't relish still sitting on the trash-strewn ground, but Lark would realize something was wrong if his legs gave out.

Lark pulled out a cell phone. "Let me call the police and an ambulance while you catch your breath."

Franklin watched her dial 911. As she grumbled her way through several automated steps, he discreetly fingered the wide silver bracelet on his right wrist. He pressed the engraving of a tiger resting under a wisteria tree, and the tree began to softly pulse with a light purple. With any luck, Harold would be there before the police.

"We're across the street from Hailey's Used Books on North Jackson." Lark looked at the alleyway's entrance. "Yes.

Thank you." As she hung up, she turned back to Franklin. "You *are* hurt!" she cried, kneeling back down next to him.

Franklin glanced down at his chest to find blood was finally soaking through his coat. "Nothing you can do," he murmured.

"We'll see," Lark said sternly. "Are you having any trouble breathing?"

"No." Franklin clenched his teeth when he shook his head. Breathing was fine for now, but any excessive movement hurt like mad.

Lark quickly felt around his head, neck, armpits, and groin area, checking to see if any blood showed up on her gloves. She seemed satisfied when they came away with no red stains.

Franklin recognized her brother's old Army backpack as she swung it around to rummage through. She looked almost exactly as she had the last time they met. Her face was more mature, filled out and refined. She was taller, and now wore a little bit of makeup. Her dark hair was still pulled back, the same baggy cargo pants, with a black leather bomber jacket covering a dark purple t-shirt. But the confident, strong air around her had not diminished in the slightest.

Finally finding a small bag with a large red cross on the side, Lark unzipped it and set it on the ground beside her. Franklin peeked in, but saw just a bundle of fabric. As Lark carefully pulled aside the left front of his jacket to see the cut on his chest, he inched his right hand toward his bag.

"Do you need something?" Lark glanced at his hand as she pulled a small pair of scissors out of her medic bag.

"I'm just thirsty." Franklin tried to sound innocent.

Lark nodded. "Just give me a minute to check this laceration, all right? Then I'll grab it for you."

Franklin relaxed.

"I'm sorry, I've got to cut your shirt to see the extent of this injury." Lark snipped away, not waiting for his agreement. "Do you hurt anywhere else?" She made quick work of wiping the blood away.

"Just some minor cuts and bruises." Aside from the poison, that was true. He was fading quickly. Pushing her hands away, Franklin grabbed his bag.

"Stop, Franklin. I still need to finish cleaning this cut," Lark softly chided.

Ignoring her, Franklin pulled the long silver bottle out of his bag, opened the lid, and threw the clear liquid at Lark with near-desperation. Most of it splashed square on her face, but the rest soaked her shirt and arms.

"What on earth?" Lark sputtered. "What was that for?"

At first, her blue and gray eyes were filled with irritation. But Franklin saw confusion creep in as she wiped her face, fingers almost completely dry. The oily substance absorbed quickly into her skin.

"What did you just throw on me?" Lark jumped up, patting down all the places the liquid was rapidly disappearing.

Distracted, Lark failed to see a flash of light behind her in the back of the alley.

Finally. Harold was here.

"Lark," Franklin whispered.

Lark's eyes narrowed in suspicion, but that was replaced with worry as she crouched down again. "Franklin? You're awfully pale. Hang on. The ambulance is coming." Her voice was fading. "Come on, please don't leave me again. I just got you back."

He stroked her face one last time. It was still such a young face. How old was she the last time they met? Seventeen? Her hand came up to gently cover his. So young, yet so strong.

His heart overflowed, but all he could manage to say with his final breath was a soft, "I'm sorry."

ϟϟϟ

Lark held Franklin's limp hand to her cheek, fighting to keep the tears at bay.

Focus! She told herself sternly. *No pulse. Get the heart pumping.*

Just as she started adjusting Franklin to lay flat on his back so she could administer CPR, Lark heard something behind her. She craned her neck to see if the EMTs had arrived without her realizing.

Seeing herself surrounded by half a dozen well-muscled men caused a stutter in her rhythmic chest compressions.

"W-who are you?" she asked, almost forgetting to resume her rescue efforts on Franklin.

One of them stepped forward and held up a box with a red cross on the side. "I'm a medic. Let me take a look?"

Lark hesitated until she noticed his silver bracelet nearly matched Franklin's. Perhaps they knew each other. She also realized if this stranger really was a certified medic, he was the best chance to save Franklin.

Stepping back, she tried to surreptitiously study the men who still surrounded her. She doubted her scrutiny went unnoticed—nothing seemed to escape their sharp gazes. These men who appeared out of nowhere all wore the same black uniform with no visible emblems or markings. Except maybe the matching silver bracelets. Unlike Franklin's, there was a larkspur blossom added to the tiger and tree design for most of the men. And these men were big. It looked like they had lived in a gym since they were ten.

One covered the prone form of the unconscious thief with what looked like a toy gun. The barrel was long and too thin to hold a bullet. Another man grabbed Lark's med kit and backpack she had forgotten next to Franklin.

"Hey, that's mine!" She started to jump forward.

The stranger to her left was on her so fast she barely had time to blink, much less yell for help, before he clamped a firm hand over her mouth. At least it was her mouth and not her throat. She couldn't afford to freeze here.

Goodness, he was fast! And strong. His arm around her midsection felt like an iron bar. Lark struggled in his grasp as hard as she could, but her captor was immovable. Was the man made of stone? Granted, her strengths–kicks and elbow strikes–were far less effective in her current position, but nothing she did seemed to have any effect on him.

"My name is Conan," the man holding her said. "I'm not going to hurt you, but I can't let you call for help, either."

Lark paused in her efforts to free herself when another man—this one with salt-and-pepper hair—kneeled next to the medic examining Franklin. He looked hopefully at the medic. "Raphael?"

The medic shook his head. "I'm sorry."

Lark's heart dropped. She barely saw the tears trickling down the face of Mr. Salt and Pepper through her own.

"I'm sorry, my friend." Mr. Salt and Pepper bowed his head.

Their whole group stilled with a heavy silence until Mr. Salt and Pepper saw Franklin's silver bottle on the ground. Carefully, he picked it up with a gloved hand and studied it. He seemed to be the one everyone was looking to for orders.

The man's head whipped toward her. "Did you drink this?" he demanded, voice strangely urgent.

Lark glared at him despite the sudden wave of nausea that washed over her.

Don't show any weakness. You're outnumbered and over-powered. Keep any advantage you have, even if it's just an illusion.

"She didn't have to drink it," Raphael said from behind Mr. Salt and Pepper. "As long as it touched her, her skin would absorb it."

All eyes turned to study Lark intently.

"How are you feeling?" Conan asked her.

Like a creepy dude is holding me prisoner and a man I used to want as a grandfather exposed me to some suspicious substance. So just grand. Thanks for asking.

Since her captor was still covering her mouth, she hoped her narrow-eyed glare at the rest of them sent her message clear enough.

Mr. Salt and Pepper gave a tight smile as a look of pity softened his brown eyes, but Lark hardly noticed the change as a horrible cramp ripped through her abdomen. She couldn't stop a groan from escaping through Conan's hand.

"We need to go." Mr. Salt and Pepper turned to the back of the alley. "It's not safe here."

Everyone started moving. Two men picked up Franklin Wright's body. Conan, maintaining his iron grip around Lark, effortlessly carried her toward a strange light at the back of the alley. A kind of muddy liquid in the shape of a rough circle splotched itself in front of the gray bricks.

Lark watched in fascinated horror as, one by one, the people in front of her walked into the now softly glowing circle. Before their figures disappeared, the strange, body-eating liquid flashed almost white before fading back to the strangely glowing muddy brown. The rough edges ebbed and flowed, but never got too small to accommodate a person.

Lark struggled again, but to no avail. Her attempted screams were still muffled by the strong hand clamped around her mouth. She didn't feel right—sick to her stomach. Cramps like a bad period, weak and shaky limbs, and a headache beginning to roar behind her eyes. But she didn't stop fighting until they got to the strange portal. Instinctively closing her eyes, she felt a momentary flash of cold. Then, the unexpected sensation of a fresh breeze on her face coaxed her eyes open.

CHAPTER 2

Instead of being surrounded by trashy stink, brick walls, and shadows, they were now in a clearing. A mountain loomed in front of them, and a lush green forest filled the peripherals of her vision. The blinding sun and sweet, sharp air almost seemed foreign. Maybe she was dreaming. Hopefully she was dreaming.

Where the heck am I?

Lark's mind couldn't catch up to what was happening. Whatever was making her feel sick must be playing tricks with her eyes as well. Even colors were...off. She couldn't quite put her finger on it, but the grass beneath her feet almost looked too green. Was that even possible? Her head felt fuzzy.

Conan had removed his hand from her mouth but still held her in his iron grip.

"W-w-what just happened?" Apparently, Lark's voice had also not caught up with the rest of her. Not that it seemed to matter, as no one bothered answering.

At the end of the clearing, she could make out a long bus surrounded by another ten or so black-clad strangers. The bus was a dark brown, with "CampCraft Rentals!" splayed across the side in bold, yellow letters.

"What's going on?" Lark hated how small her voice was. She cleared her throat. "Who are you people?"

No one answered her as they walked toward the group surrounding the bus and what looked like motorcycles on the side of the road. Mr. Salt and Pepper stopped Conan and another of his men halfway toward the dirt road.

He handed the young soldier a syringe, then turned to Lark. "Forgive us, but time is short, and our priority is to keep you safe; I know no other way, considering your frame of mind. You need rest for the bonding. All will be explained as soon as we are in a safer position."

With that, he strode toward the larger group, talking in urgent tones with another one of his men.

Lark stared after him, uncomprehending. Her thoughts were mush, and Mr. Salt and Pepper wasn't making any sense. She watched him gesture with short, anxious movements from the waiting group toward the mountain. They all wore the same plain black uniforms, and everyone sported holstered guns—some on their hips, some strapped to their thighs or calves. Lark focused her tired gaze on the young man still in front of her, the one with the syringe.

He stepped forward with regret in his eyes. "I'm sorry."

When Lark's muddled mind finally realized she was going to be injected with something, adrenaline momentarily suppressed her nausea and sent strength surging into her shaky limbs.

"No!" she shrieked, kicking out her right leg. Her foot hit the man square in the chest, the force sending him sprawling.

Lark was not the only one surprised at the success of her attack. Conan loosened his concentration and grip just enough for her to squirm out of his grasp at last. She spun and sprinted past Conan, realizing the muddy liquid they just walked through had disappeared. Instead, her eyes zeroed in on the man holding her backpack.

Lunging toward him, she threw her elbow, smashing it into his jaw. He stumbled back, and she wrenched her backpack from his grasp.

"Sorry!" she called back, heart thudding wildly as she sprinted for the cover of the trees, ignoring the calls that followed her. She chided herself for feeling bad about leaving the guys sprawled like that. Why should she feel guilty? They were the ones who had kidnapped her. She was totally justified...*ugh*. "Sorry," she whispered again.

Sometimes, she really wanted to smack herself.

Trying to keep the weakness from creeping back into her legs, she ran blindly through the trees. What was in the water Franklin threw on her?

She finally stopped when she stumbled over something and nearly fell flat on her face. She stared with horror at the large dead animal in front of her. Then confusion warred with horror as she realized the animal was a tiger.

What was a tiger doing in a forest? She looked around, confirming she was indeed in a forest, not a jungle. Trees were not her area of expertise, but she did know you didn't usually find pine and oak trees in a jungle.

The tiger's body was destroyed with burns and covered in blood, apparently making the fur useless. The sick poachers had only taken the head. The gruesome sight and the stench of death combined with her upset stomach, making Lark want to heave. She took a few precious moments to take some deep breaths and push down the threatening nausea.

Just as she prepared to run again, she heard a soft cry from a cluster of nearby rocks. She took an involuntary step toward the noise, her heartstrings plucking painfully.

No, Lark. She turned resolutely away. *You've got to get out of here!*

She could already hear the troop coming after her, but she couldn't walk away from the plaintive mewling that started up again.

After touching the dog tags tucked under her shirt, Lark followed the cries and discovered a small burrow below an overhanging rock. She peered in and saw the most adorable fluffball of a white tiger cub hunched up.

She rested her backpack against the rock before coaxing the cub out, not without a few bites and scratches. The cub was so tiny. Lark wasn't sure it was even weaned yet.

"Oh, poor baby. You're all alone too, aren't you? This must have been your mama."

The struggle with Lark seemed to have completely exhausted the small, female cub. With a weak cry, she stopped struggling, either understanding she was safe with this new creature or too exhausted to fight anymore.

When she blinked light blue eyes at Lark, the feline and human sighed together. Lark wasn't sure why, but having the cub curl up in her arms felt necessary somehow—it felt right. Even her nausea subsided a bit.

In that moment, she realized how lonely she had become. Staying busy with work and school had been a way to help ease the sting of being on her own for several years, but it could never heal the wounds.

Conan, leading a couple other men, emerged from the trees.

Lark glared at him defiantly.

"Please." He sounded frustrated.

Join the club, bud.

"I know it's hard to imagine right now, but we want to help you." Conan's voice softened a touch.

Lark knew she couldn't outrun them now. Her head was pounding too much to run anymore.

"You won't hurt her?" she asked, cradling the cub protectively. There was no logical reason for it, but Lark's heart rate spiked just thinking about anything happening to the cub.

"We wouldn't dream of it." Conan promised.

Lark took a hesitant step closer. "Is someone going to give me some answers soon?"

"Once you've had some rest. You don't look like you can stand much longer." He gave what was probably the most concerned look she had seen on his face yet.

He was probably right. Her adrenaline was spent, and more soldiers had circled behind. All of them looked at the mother tiger. Lark was surprised to see anger, disgust, and a little bit of worry in their glances. She didn't have time to figure out how she felt about that.

Conan held out his arm. "Please. We must hurry."

Lark took a deep breath before allowing herself to be escorted back to the clearing, hugging the now-sleeping cub to herself.

CHAPTER 3

"**W**here is It?" Casimer Talbot thundered.

The forty-year-old man's copper irises narrowed in anger, making his angular face look even sharper. His thinning hair was short, forest green curls.

He stood in his luxurious office. A desk made of light wood and a matching chair were ornately decorated with delicate scrollwork. Both rested beneath a round window overlooking a small garden. One entire wall of the white-washed room had been left unadorned so he could project the TV onto it anytime he wanted. The others were covered with maps, pictures of his dead parents, and family crests.

With a grunt, Casimer ground his heel into the lush carpet and threw his purple cloak onto the back of the chair with a swish. The color usually soothed him. It reminded him that he was of royal blood, entitled to anything he wanted.

"It's been a week since Aldwin's idiots attacked Franklin. Avi would have tried to retrieve him already!"

Casimer's commander general, Beck Jones, cleared his throat. "We set up surveillance teams near the most likely particle collection points they would use. We're pretty sure a group of Wysteria Corps gathered in Orville, which is near one of the spots they could initiate a time slip." The tall, muscular thirty-year-old looked at Casimer with slightly glassy blue eyes.

Casimer frowned. If only Aldwin hadn't moved too early. His men didn't have the equipment to follow Franklin into the past.

"I don't know if they will opt for speed or secrecy," Beck said, rubbing his chin with a hand tanned from hours of training in the sun. "If it's speed, they'll take the sky trams back to Vusal."

"If secrecy, they'll head through the forest reserve," Casimer mused. "Steele set up there, correct?"

"Yes sir." Beck nodded. "He's based between three different points we thought they might use for time travel."

"Have him send out scouts in case Avi sends them that way. And make sure we have people on every sky tram from Orville to Vusal until we find them."

"Yes sir."

Beck left to distribute his orders.

As Casimer sank into the chair, his thin face pinched even more with worry. His...*associate*...would not be happy with this turn of events. Doctor Wright was part of their deal. He was now going to have to sacrifice more of his own progress than anticipated. Casimer couldn't afford to lose their help, but he was sure they would use this opportunity to demand something more of him.

Life is lonely when you can't trust anyone.

"Are you feeling all right?"

Lark stopped trudging with her head hanging and glanced up to see Mr. Salt and Pepper holding out a steadying hand, studying her with concern.

She had refused to let anyone touch or help her as she followed Conan back to the clearing, though she had allowed him to carry the backpack she laid aside while getting the cub out of her hiding place. She wouldn't normally let a stranger touch it, but in this case, it was hard enough just standing.

Lark had spent the first part of their walk back trying to figure out why her condition was so bad. Was it a reaction to being exposed to whatever Franklin had thrown on her earlier? But the nausea, shaking, sweating, and headache kept getting worse until she could no longer wonder and had to save all her energy for moving forward.

Mr. Salt and Pepper searched her face with hopeful expectancy. "I am Commander General Harold Cynbel. Was Doctor Wright able to tell you about me? About anything?"

Lark hesitated. Her throat was parched, and she was having a difficult time remembering anything. She shook her head slowly.

If her eyes would stop swimming, she would try to take in more of her surroundings. As it was, she sifted through some of her other senses. There was a clean, woodsy scent on the air, although she wasn't sure if that was a lingering memory from her bout in the woods. The packed dirt road they were on was rougher on her feet than the grassy clearing or soft forest floor.

The men she could see glanced at each other uneasily. Mr. Sal—the commander general—appeared disappointed.

"You need some rest, then I will answer as many questions as I can." Commander General Cynbel led her toward the bus.

Lark was anxious for answers, but part of her also wanted to stay in delusional denial about whatever was happening. She almost hoped she would simply wake up in her bed, ready to bore herself with studying for medical exams.

Her urge to run away from all this warred against the stubborn part of her that wanted to keep going and see where this led. The strangers treated her with respect, as if they actually cared about her. It had been a long time since anyone cared what happened to her.

Of course, they *had* taken her against her will through a splotchy wall and tried to inject her with some unknown... something. Maybe they weren't such great guys after all.

Lark shook her head. Sometimes she forgot that her spiky personality and carefully constructed barriers she forged were in reality closer to a paper-thin veneer than iron-clad barricades.

I know I've been on my own for a while, but being lonely is probably not a good reason to make friends with people who can walk through a wall and come out in a forest.

"Miss Lark." Commander General Cynbel opened a door near the front of the bus and held out his hand to help Lark up the steps.

Lark tried to scowl at him. It wasn't easy, considering she could hardly feel her facial muscles, but she gave it a try anyway. Weird, since every other muscle seemed to be screaming at her. "How do you know my name?"

"Would you prefer Larkspur?" Mr. Salt and Pepper asked. Lark decided to keep the nickname, frustrated that he didn't seem to be inclined to answer her questions.

She wanted to keep pressing. She didn't want to look like a gullible, apologetic woman. But darn it, old habits die hard. That, and she could barely keep on her feet. She just didn't have the strength to fight for answers right now.

She sighed. "Lark or Larkspur. Whichever you prefer. I don't care."

The last thing she saw was a small smile on Mr. Salt and Pepper's face before her vision went black and her knees buckled. She heard muffled voices over the ringing in her ears. Someone picked her up and carefully set her down on something soft, where she finally fell into a fevered sleep, the tiger cub still slumbering in her arms.

ᔦᔦᔦ

Conan joined Shamira Alfhard as she watched over Lark's fitful slumber. "How is she doing?"

"She's feverish." Sharmia turned to look at her commander, wiping a lock of fiery red hair out of her eyes. "I can't quite tell if she's bothered by physical pain or some sort of mental distress." Her voice carried the same tone of worry she saw written on Conan's face.

Conan lifted a bloodied piece of cloth Shamira had tossed aside, glancing at her bandaged hands.

"Ah." Shamira gave a light snort. "The little cub. She objects to being separated. And they both seem to find comfort with each other."

Conan nodded, then gave his cropped dark blond hair a nervous rub. "Is there anything else we can do?"

Shamira considered the question as she wiped Lark's forehead of sweat. "Honestly, not even Raphael knows what she needs. I wish your brother was here. With Director Wright dead, we have no one here who fully understands..." Shamira's voice trailed off with a meaningful look that traveled from the fitfully-sleeping Lark to the front of the vacation bus where Franklin's body was stored.

"No one expected..." Conan's voice faded as sorrow filled his eyes.

"I'm sorry," Shamira said softly. "I know you were all close." Her eyes fell on the tiny tiger cub. "Who would have thought the heir would stumble across a tiger right after coming here?" She shook her head, smiling incredulously. "Like it was meant to be."

"No one will contest her rule, considering the cub seems to already be so attached to her." Conan's tone was guarded.

Lots of opinions had swirled about the unknown heir to Lothar's throne, but Commander Conan had always remained mute on the subject.

"At least not openly," Shamira agreed. "I think they both needed someone," she added quietly.

Conan furrowed his brow. "The tiger can't be more than two months old. Look at how small she is. She's going to need a lot of care to survive."

Shamira and Conan tensed as Lark started tossing and turning, nearly crushing the tiger in the midst of her flailing.

"Grab the cub!" Conan cried, coming beside Lark to try and steady her.

Lark calmed for a moment before her eyes flew open and a cry of pain tore from her lips.

"I've got you," Conan soothed, cooling her head with a wet towel.

"Raphael!" Shamira yelled for their unit's medical officer while filling a nearby cup with water. "Try to drink," Shamira told Lark as she handed Conan the cup and then refocused her attention on the unhappy cub's yowls.

Lark only swallowed a few sips before she was again overpowered by spasms just as Raphael entered the halted bus.

"Conan—I mean, commander!" Shamira nodded with a slight tremor toward Lark's clenched fists.

The soft blankets bunched in her hands were scorched.

"Commander general!" Conan shouted.

Within seconds Commander General Cynbel lunged into the bus. He just as swiftly disappeared out the door again. "Get her out here while I activate my Fire Suit. Quickly!"

Shamira followed Raphael and Conan as they carried Lark out of the bus, the tiger still complaining in her arms.

The commander general whispered into his bracelet before a wave spread across his uniform, the black cloth swiftly turning into a bulky, one-piece fire suit.

"Bring water," Raphael ordered.

"Here." Shamira shoved the wailing white ball of fluff into the closest soldier's hands and dove back onto the bus.

᚛᚛᚛

The pain came in waves.

Lark's vision kept going funny. She thought she smelled smoke, and once, she tossed her arm, and it looked like she had cracked a tree trunk.

Great. Now I'm hallucinating. Wait. Since when was I napping under a tree?

Bleary eyed, Lark glanced around. She leaned against Mr. Salt and Pepper, who sat underneath a tree with branches full of large white leaves.

Wait, what? White leaves? But there's no snow on the ground, and it's not cold. Quite the opposite.

Resolutely looking away from the branches, Lark decided not to think about that for now. Attempting to shift to a sitting position, Lark's attention was brought back to Mr. Salt and Pepper. Whatever he was wearing was hard and uncomfortable to her over-sensitized skin.

What was his name again? Commander...something or other? Or was it general?

This has to be a dream, she told herself, reflexively accepting continuous sips of water. *But I'd really like this dream to end!* She wanted to cry as a new influx of pain crashed down on her.

The only reason she didn't face plant into the grass was thanks to Mr. Salt and Pepper's arms holding her up. He gently pulled her back so she was resting against him again. His gloved hand smoothing her dark, sweat-soaked hair was soothing, lulling her delirious mind toward sleep as the pain dulled.

She gave a weak smile. "Thank you, Mr. Salt and Pepper." Lark reached up to pat his cropped locks.

His eyes widened, flabbergasted amusement on his face. The warning look he threw toward the coughs and snorts Lark heard spring up around them contrasted sharply with the soft smile he turned on her.

"Are you feeling better?" he asked in such a fatherly voice that it nearly brought tears to her eyes. He looked about the right age to be her father, maybe forty or fifty, but she hadn't had great experiences with her own father, so she didn't dwell on the thought.

"I don't...understand..." her words slurred as she fought to keep her eyes focused.

"I can answer some of your questions, but only when you've gotten a bit of sleep."

Lark wanted to protest, but she couldn't seem to keep her eyes open.

Maybe just a short nap.

CHAPTER 4

Harold Cynbel carried Lark's sleeping form back to the bus.

Conan fell in step beside him. "Sir, are you all right?" He nodded to some burn marks on Harold's suit and to where Lark had struck him with her fevered flailing.

"The suit did its job," Harold said. "I might have a few bruises, but nothing a little time won't cure. She was close enough that her hits didn't have very much momentum behind them."

"It's a good thing you had the suit programmed in the nano-cloth. Not knowing what to expect made preparations difficult." Conan sighed.

Harold gave him an understanding smile. The Spur Corps was Conan's most important command, and it came with unprecedented difficulties. "We'll stop at the river. It means we won't get much farther today, but I don't want to be close to anyone until she's stable. Franklin said the bonding would take several hours. We'll have enough juice to get the vacation bus back in time."

Conan gave a stiff salute. "Yes sir, Mr. Salt and Pepper, sir!"

Harold clamped down on the amusement in his chest so he could narrow his eyes in annoyance at his eldest son. "Conan Cynbel," he said warningly.

"I'll go relay your orders, sir!" Conan scampered off with a laugh.

Harold harrumphed, more to hide his own laughter than anything else. He then carefully brought Lark back onto the bus and carried her past the chairs in the front, the mini table and kitchen, the bathroom, eventually gently depositing her in what he hoped was a comfortable position on the bed. "Shamira, Raphael," he called.

"Sir." Shamira followed the medic onto the bus, again holding the tiger cub and reminding Harold about the extra, unexpected responsibility.

The cub had given the occasional pitiful yowl, but it grew into a constant, keening whine as soon as she spotted Lark asleep on the bed.

Shamira gave him a look that was half questioning, half pleading. "Commander general? What do we do with this little one? She only seems to want Larkspur, but she needs to eat eventually."

"I remember reading somewhere that in ancient times camel's milk was used for lots of different species that still needed their mother's milk but couldn't get it." Raphael offered.

"But we don't have camel's milk," Shamira reminded him. "We don't even know if she's still supposed to have milk."

Harold held out his arms. "I'll see what I can find for this little girl. Raphael, if she needs it, help Shamira clean the princess." To give them a few minutes of privacy, Harold moved forward in the bus to the tiny kitchenette to rummage through their limited supplies. Not entirely sure what such a tiny cub would need, Harold finally settled on some water and jerky before heading back.

The tiger insisted on staying by Larkspur, so Harold fed the hungry cub next to the sleeping girl.

Without waking up, Lark shifted so she was facing him. Even in her sleep, she didn't expose her back, not that he blamed her. She probably hadn't been given much reason to trust in her short twenty years. But everything was changing now.

He looked down at her with a mixture of affection and worry. She was near the age of his sons. If his daughter had lived, she would have been only a few years younger than Lark.

Yes, for better or worse, everything had changed. Lark was a new and different person in a new and different world.

Harold just hoped she could forgive them for that.

Lark woke up to semi-darkness. She sat up, careful not to wake the sleeping tiger.

Wait, tiger? That wasn't all a dream?

She hesitantly stroked the soft fur. Nope, that felt pretty real.

Lark looked at her surroundings. The bed she was laying on felt like a cloud, piled with soft blankets and pillows. It extended all the way to cushioned walls along the sides and head. The foot of the bed opened up into a short, dark hallway.

That bus I saw earlier must have been an RV.

Lark peered into the dark ahead of her. It wasn't until she crawled off the bed that the realization hit her—she was clean, wearing comfortable, purple silk pajamas that were lined with a delicate lace she wouldn't normally even entertain looking at in a store.

Her heart skipped a beat and her hands flew to the dog tags still laying around her neck. She tried to remember anything at all after she patted Mr. Salt and Pepper's hair.

Oh, gosh. She covered her face in embarrassment. *I really wish that had been a dream.*

She checked herself to make sure she was all right, but nothing seemed amiss. If anything, she felt amazing. Rested and energized.

Since she couldn't find her old clothes, she grabbed her backpack from the foot of the bed and quickly changed into the spare clothes she kept there. She studied her pocketknife before slipping it into the front pocket of her cargo pants.

Lark tiptoed her way toward what she assumed was the front of the RV. Past the tiny toilet, a pantry stuffed with food that made her empty stomach grumble, and a small table. Her eyes had adjusted well enough that she clearly recognized Franklin's body stretched out on a couch.

She couldn't keep the tears back as she remembered his last moments and her powerlessness to help him. Wiping her eyes clear, she peered at him. Lark didn't know how long she had been out, but Franklin looked remarkably well-preserved. She glanced around to make sure no one was watching, and then reached out to touch his face.

There was some sort of plastic covering his body. It clung to him like a second skin. That must be keeping the smell and decomposition process at bay until they reached their destination. Wherever that was.

Trailing her fingers down Franklin's plastic-covered cheek in a sad farewell, Lark moved on. She was now at the front of the bus. All the windows were covered. She found the door but paused with her hand resting on the handle. She pulled aside the corner of the curtain and peeked out before barging into the open.

It was still dark outside. A fire crackled away, maybe a bus length from the door, and a few people sat and chatted around the flames, but Lark barely paid them any heed.

The blaze was mesmerizing. Red-hot coals in the base turned into a fluid yellow and orange flame, which in turn licked its way into the air before dissolving away into magical little embers. It was beautiful. Pulled at her. Called—

"Larkspur?"

Lark yelped in surprise, stumbled, and fell forward into soft grass.

Grass? When did I open the door?

Lark looked around in confusion. Since when had she left the bus?

Mr. Salt and Pepper had apparently been standing guard next to the door. He came over to help Lark to her feet. She brushed imaginary grass and dirt from her legs, too embarrassed to look up.

"I apologize for scaring you," Mr. Salt and Pepper said. "Are you all right?"

"I think so." She finally looked at him.

One of his eyebrows raised in surprise when he saw her face.

Realizing he was still gently holding onto her hand, Lark snatched it back, questions about what they had done to her still on her mind.

"Thank you," she said stiffly.

"Ah." His voice carried a warm note of understanding. "After you passed out, Shamira cleaned and changed you so you would be comfortable. Nothing more."

Lark narrowed her eyes, then nodded.

"Are you thirsty?" Harold handed over a canteen.

Lark hesitated for a moment and fingered her knife, then decided to give him a chance. Right now, she needed answers. If she needed to escape later, she would find her opportunities. She accepted the canteen, taking a small sip at first and letting the water sit in her mouth as she looked around, trying desperately to ignore the pull of the fire.

Soft starlight showed silhouettes of surrounding trees. A river softly murmured nearby. A chorus of crickets and frogs came from the surrounding darkness. The handful of people she could see had some sort of jacket on, so Lark was surprised to find the weather didn't feel cold to her.

"Thank you—I'm sorry, I don't remember your rank. Commander? Or was it general?" Lark passed the canteen back after drinking her fill.

"Commander General Harold Cynbel. But Harold is fine. I prefer that to Salt and Pepper," he laughed.

Lark winced in embarrassment then cleared her throat. "Thank you for helping me."

Harold gave a small nod.

Feeling awkward, Lark started walking to give her legs a stretch. And to get away from that fire. Mr. Sal—er, Harold, accompanied her silently.

"Where are we?" Lark finally decided to start with this question out of the thousands running around in her head.

Despite being slightly overcast, a fair amount of starlight pierced the foliage they had meandered under. Or maybe dawn was starting to break? Her vision had significantly improved since waking up. They were far away from the warmth and light of the campfire.

Harold took a deep breath. "A better question might be *when* are we."

They had walked down to the river. Lark stopped by the bank. The water was so clear that she was able to see dark shapes of fish. Some longer fleeting shadows she could only assume were otters darted around the occasional boulder. She had been stuck in cities for far too long. She missed the good, clean smell of the woods. The spicy scent of pines carried on the cool breeze. Lark took a deep breath.

Then Harold's words registered.

"I beg your pardon?"

"This is going to be difficult to accept, but we are two thousand years in the future. On the planet Evren, in the Verne solar system."

"Right..." Lark said slowly, then shook her head. "I'm sorry, could you run that by me again?" So much for giving the guy a chance.

"The year is 4023."

Lark looked around as if to find evidence of a different planet. Nothing looked out of the ordinary. Well, come to think of it, the colors did look a little off. But maybe that was just predawn playing tricks on her?

She crossed her arms, an action not entirely lost in the semi-darkness. "You seriously expect me to believe we just traveled in time and space?"

"What do you think the portal we went through was?"

"I don't know." Lark was frustrated. "Some top secret government teleportation device?"

Oh yes, that's a much better explanation. Lark rolled her eyes.

Dawn started to light the sky.

"Well, time travel did sort of stem from that." Harold conceded. "But teleportation wasn't perfected until 2510, and this planet wasn't terraformed until 3745. Time travel is still very new. Only within the last five years has Professor Wright been able to crack—"

Harold was cut off by a commotion behind them. Motors grumbling, the sound of feet running, and yelling.

"What's going on?" Lark turned around.

Conan came loping toward them. "Robbers." He sounded more annoyed than worried. In fact, he looked remarkably relaxed about the fact that they were being attacked.

"My trauma kit is in the RV!" Lark started going back up the path toward the campsite, where screams could now be heard.

Conan blocked her way. "There's no need."

"But—"

"Raphael can help anyone who needs it." Conan turned to Harold. "Faolan said he recognized a couple of the kids from when he rented the vacation bus. It seems to be some sort of gang initiation."

Lark gawked as a motor roared up behind Conan. "Is that...is that a, a motorcycle that's *hovering?*"

Conan grunted something that might have been a curse under his breath as he threw himself onto Lark when the hovering aggressor produced a gun and pulled the trigger. His force sent them both tumbling to the ground. Lark landed on her back and gaped in disbelief as a blue energy blast, not a bullet, spat from the gun.

Harold pulled his own weapon and fired a white-hot laser beam at the assailant, who fell instantly. The bike stopped and remained hovering with a soft whir next to its fallen rider.

Unfortunately, Harold wasn't quick enough to stop part of the blast from hitting Conan, who was still covering Lark.

"Conan!" Lark wriggled out from under his fallen form.

She might not trust these guys, or even like them, but that didn't mean she wanted any of them to get shot by scary blue lasers. Especially if they were protecting her from the blast. She stared at Conan's wound. She had studied a lot for her upcoming medical exams, but she had never read about a wound that glowed before.

What the heck am I supposed to do with this? Is it radioactive?

Harold kneeled beside them and talked into his bracelet. Footsteps came up behind them and Lark tried to turn around, but her attention was arrested by the blue energy glowing from the burn on Conan's chest.

Why can't I stop looking at it? Fear creeped in when she got the urge to touch it. *Wait for Raphael! He's the trained professional.* But it was no use. As Harold was distracted with whoever was coming from the campsite, Lark's hand reached out on its own.

"No, don't touch it!" Conan managed to wheeze.

That brought everyone's attention to her, but it was too late. The glowing blue energy started to float from Conan's chest to Lark's hand. At the same time, a strange tingling started in her arm, then progressed all over. She stared, transfixed, as her skin changed. Not only was the color turning an opaque black, but it was also changing texture. It hardened into something like armor. Armor that was a part of her.

"What's happening?" she cried out as the energy continued to leave Conan and enter her. "Harold?"

The handful of people who had gathered watched as if hypnotized, but Lark's scared, small voice calling Harold's name seemed to jerk him out of his trance. Lark stood, all the blue energy gone. But she shook violently, a thousand new questions screaming in her head.

"It's all right." Harold took a step toward her, the want to comfort and protect her evident on his face.

"No! Don't touch me." She jumped back. "I don't want to accidentally hurt you. What is going on?"

Harold opened his mouth, but nothing came out.

"What is happening to me?" Lark nearly screamed.

"Our planet was under threat of invasion." Harold slowly began. "Doctor Franklin Wright set about trying to create something that would help. The result was something like a nano-byte. Biological Mutation Bytes. His pet name for them was bio-bots. My limited understanding is that millions of these tiny, partially organic inventions could be programmed to bond with one person, becoming part of their physical makeup, giving them certain abilities. That person is you."

Lark's head spun. She couldn't very well deny the validity of his statement. She had lived through it.

That's what was in the water you threw on me? Lark railed to Franklin. *How could you do that to me?*

As she watched her hands turn back to their original color, icy fear gripped her heart. Her whole body still felt odd. Like her skin was just a little too tight.

"How do I get rid of it?" she tried to ask calmly. As if she was going to quietly accept an alien invasion in her own body!

Everyone shuffled uneasily, but no one said anything.

"Somebody answer!" Lark didn't care about how much her voice shook. "When did 'the powers that be' decide all this? No one asked if *I* wanted any part of it. I don't want any 'certain abilities.' At least not until they're explained to me. How do I get this to stop? Get rid of these...things?"

Harold's answer sent a hammer through her chest.

"You can't get rid of them, Larkspur," he said quietly; apologetically. "It's impossible to separate the bio-bots from your genetic makeup. But even if it were possible, they can only bond with one person's DNA. Dr. Franklin and King Avi chose you. I'm sorry."

"No, no, no." Lark threw the men around her accusatory glares before whirling around to stumble blindly through the trees. She wasn't trying to run away again, although she wanted to. But really, where would she go? She was lost, two thousand years in the future. Or still in the middle of a horrible dream.

She needed some space and time to think. Try to wrap her head around everything.

CHAPTER 5

Harold watched Lark stalk away into the trees. He was tired. So tired. And this journey had only just begun.

"Have Shamira lead a couple men to follow and protect, but from a distance. She needs time," he ordered before turning back to Conan and Raphael.

Conan's gaze followed Lark's disappearing figure with a severe expression. "Will she be all right?"

Harold realized all of his men were waiting intently for his answer.

"I'm not sure," he answered truthfully. "But can you blame her? She's been through so much. Too much. All we can do is wait and be here when she is ready to accept us. For the moment, let's make sure you are going to be all right."

"She did the hard part," Raphael said with awe. "There's no trace of blue rad!"

Normally, getting rid of the radiation from a laser wound was a difficult, time-intensive process, even from the less harmful colors, like blue and green. Lark had gotten rid of it all within a few minutes.

"Now it's just a regular burn, and that is easily healed. You'll be good as new in no time." Raphael finished putting a clear gel on Conan's burns and helped him up.

"Thanks, doc," Conan grunted as he stood straight.

"You should be thanking the princess." Raphael shook his head. "I didn't know she'd be able to do that."

"Neither did I," Harold said with a frown. "I wish..." He let his sentence hang as his gaze fell on the bus where Franklin Wright's body was secured. "Interesting times are ahead of us."

"Da—sir." Conan corrected himself as they made their way back to the campsite. "What if she refuses? What if she really does say no? Where will that leave us?"

"I'm not sure it leaves us very far behind where we are now. What did they expect?" Harold growled. "She was supposed to be the test. A prototype. The first of a *team*. But without Franklin, she's alone. At least for now. As powerful as she is, she's just one person." It was difficult keeping a tired note out of his voice. "It is possible the princess may choose to ignore her new life. Although I doubt she could completely. She's a natural-born healer. She simply can't ignore anyone in need. But she will, eventually, have to accept the fact that she's a different person with new abilities."

᚛᚛᚛

Nearly two hundred yards away, Lark was coming to the same conclusion.

Surrounded by a wide circle of protection from the guards, she paced back and forth, circling trees, clenching the dog tags around her neck, and muttering to herself for who knew how long.

Which, she realized, was getting her nowhere.

If what Harold said was true, then she was stuck with these people for the foreseeable future.

"The future. Ha!" Lark said. "That suddenly has a whole new meaning." She gave a short, humorless laugh.

She furrowed her brow as she stared unhappily at the grass. *What is wrong with my eyesight?* The color seemed a bit off. Squinting at her forest surroundings, the greens looked richer, darker than she remembered leaves looking. *What have these crazy bio-bot things done to me?*

Frustrated, she punched the thick trunk of a nearby tree. Splinters flew everywhere as her right arm buried itself in the wood halfway up to her elbow. The bones in her hand and arm crunched. She gasped in surprise and pain. But not nearly as much pain as she should be in. Why wasn't she screaming in agony? She carefully extracted her arm from the tree.

The grass rustled behind her and she whirled around to face several approaching guards.

"I'm fine!" she snapped, not wanting to see anyone right now, no matter how bad her hand was. She knew she shouldn't be angry at the poor soldiers who were only trying to follow orders and protect her. It wasn't their fault she was in this situation, as far as she knew. But she was too confused to care.

She glanced down at her arm. And then did a double take.

Oh. Maybe I spoke too soon.

She bled where splinters of bone peeked from the skin of her forearm and her fingers were bent in unnatural positions. What wasn't there was the torment that usually accompanied an injury such as this.

Wailing did finally register through the shock, but it wasn't from her. Lark glanced up to see the tiger cub struggling in the arms of a tall woman with fiery red hair and eyes that looked just like emeralds. Her arms were covered in something thick like leather. A good thing, or they would have been shredded with the fuss the cub was making.

Heart melting, Lark took the cub with her good arm. "I'm sorry, girl," she cooed softly.

The tiger immediately stopped crying. She happily used Lark's arm as a climbing post and made herself comfortable on Lark's shoulder. With the occasional whine, she gently pawed at Lark's injury.

The woman with hair like fire stared at Lark's eyes, which irritated her. But before she barked at the stranger, Lark's arm began to buzz and tingle. Both women's eyes glued to the phenomenon happening in Lark's body. Her skin turned slightly opaque as her arm started to heal from the inside out. Fingers snapped back into place with a sickening crunch, bones disappeared back under the skin as her arm straightened out and closed any lacerations.

Lark wiped the blood to reveal baby-new skin. She looked up to meet emerald eyes as wide as her own.

How many more surprises were in store for her? Her skin still felt tight, her strength had grown, and now she apparently had healing abilities. Would she continue to get stronger? Was her eyesight actually messed up? What limitations did she have now?

I need—

A silky tail flicked in her face, interrupting her panicked thoughts.

Right. Calm down. First things first.

Where could she go? She knew nothing about this place. What would she do? Keep running and hiding, finding out new abilities by accident? Come to think of it, hadn't the commander general called the planet something different? It started with an E, she was fairly certain. Evren? Everett? Whatever he called it, it wasn't Earth. Was the wildlife different on this planet? Maybe she didn't know poisonous from safe in this place.

Harold and his men were the only ones she knew around here with any answers. Actually, they were the only ones she knew, period. She was a stranded loner, out of place, and out of time. Literally.

"Um, miss?" Lark finally asked the red-haired woman still slack jawed in front of her.

"Colonel Shamira Alfhard!" The woman stiffened to attention.

"Uh, colonel." Lark gave an awkward nod in acknowledgment. "If you wouldn't mind leading the way, we should probably head back."

Shamira relaxed, looking relieved. "This way."

As Lark followed Shamira, the tiger cub still contentedly riding her shoulders, she couldn't help flexing her right hand and arm. There wasn't any pain, which in and of itself was unbelievable. The other weird thing was her skin still felt tight all over, and she wanted to keep rubbing her eyes because everything seemed...off. She couldn't put her finger on what, exactly, but nothing looked quite right.

When they finally reached the campsite, Lark stopped short.

"The bus." She couldn't stop staring. "It's...flying? Floating?"

"Hovering," Sharmira corrected her. "It's a vacation bus."

"So, not just bikes, but buses...hover...here." Lark blinked.

Shamira smiled. "Yes, although you'll see a lot more in a city. They have to stay near a Hewa Battery, or else hovercrafts take over a day to recharge."

Lark nodded, pretending to understand. She'd figure the whole hover thing out later. Right now, she had caught sight of Harold. Before she could even think about going home, she needed some answers.

"So basically, I'm a secret prototype superhuman weapon. And the only person who actually knows what to expect, or could make more people like me, is dead. Leaving me stranded in not only a different time period, but a whole new solar system. My day just keeps getting..." Lark cut herself off with a frustrated grunt.

She and Harold sat near the front of the vacation bus on cushioned chairs that faced the couch on which Franklin's body was laid out. After the tiger cub kept trying to go over and scratch at the preservation plastic over him, Lark eventually plopped the cub in her lap where she finally curled up to take a nap. Conan rested on a chair next to Franklin's couch.

"That's not entirely accurate." Harold shook his head. "Franklin's death has complicated matters, but there is someone who should be able to make something similar.

You are not a weapon for someone's use, and you were never meant to be the only one."

Lark gave him a look that said, "*How dumb do you think I am?*"

"At least, that was not the intention. I suppose a bit of that is unavoidable," he conceded thoughtfully. "But we don't need a secret weapon. What we need is someone who can unify the land. The bio-bots were designed to help the person protect, not destroy. That's why we looked for someone with a strong heart to heal. It's a high compliment that Doctor Wright and King Avi thought you could do it."

"Wait. Avi Kynaston was a king? Like, Majesty, royal palaces, thrones and stuff? For real?" Lark thought of the graying man with the laughing eyes.

"He *is* a real king, yes. Our king. That's who we're taking you to," said Harold.

Lark thought back to three years ago. Or, at least, three years of her life ago.

CHAPTER 6

⌛ ⌛ ⌛

Lark's brothers were overseas on a tour. She was missing them, so packed up the extra army backpack they gave her with supplies for a day at the beach. A thirty-minute Jet Ski ride brought her to one of their favorite spots—an isolated cove where she learned to swim the first time they lived in this area.

She shared many fond memories of that cove with her brothers. But that day, she wasn't left in peace for very long to ruminate on them.

Lark began dozing off, basking in the sunshine, when she heard angry voices coming from the other side of the rock outcrop she was lying next to. Annoyed that her refuge of solitude was being encroached upon, she got ready to move farther down the beach. But she went stock-still as the voices became clear on the wind.

"It's a little hard to concentrate with your weapons in my face. It's right around here. Just give me a minute."

That was the first time Lark heard Franklin Wright's voice.

At seventeen, Lark was much more naive. Heedless of her own safety, she would rush in to help wherever there was a need without thinking. And there was a need now; that much was clear.

She quietly scaled the rocks and carefully peeked over the top. An old man searched the rocks opposite her. Between them, there was a small grassy area ending in a short, one-meter cliff into the deep blue ocean. On the grass stood three men, two with rifles slung on their sides, hands at the ready to bring them up for firing. Everyone's backs were turned toward Lark.

"Remember, if we are not back within an hour, my men *will* kill Avi," the leader threatened. Lark assumed he was the leader because he was the only one without a weapon drawn, and he wore an odd purple cape that distinguished him from everyone else.

"As you have told me several times, Casimer," Franklin said in a tired voice. "I can't believe you would go to these lengths. Betraying your own uncle, all for what, power you've never even tried to earn?" Franklin turned to glower at him.

Then he locked eyes with Larkspur.

Fortunately, no one seemed to notice his eyes widen, nor ask why he whirled back around to keep searching the rocks.

"That power belongs to me. He has no right to give it away!" Casimer snarled.

Lark ducked back behind the rocks, heart pounding. She had talked through hundreds of survival and rescue scenarios with Alex and Sterling since that was their job in the Army, but it was all theory. This was real life. People's lives were in danger!

Think, Lark! What's the point of training and learning everything from Lex and Sterl if you can't actually use it?

She took a couple deep breaths, then weighed her options. The police were severely understaffed in this city. Almost every call took at least an hour for anyone to respond to. And they were way out on a mostly deserted stretch of beach. The closest house was several hundred yards away. The family she was staying with while her brothers were deployed couldn't help—they were out of town for the rest of the week. Lark had stayed behind because her family's home goods were being picked up later that day for their move next month.

Okay. So backup was probably not going to get there in time to help. This Casimer guy had said an hour, but one of them might get a little trigger-happy sooner rather than later.

She retreated to grab her stun gun and pocketknife from her backpack, then rummaged around in the seat of her Jet Ski just in case there was something there that could help. There was a tiny first aid kit and—a flare gun! She had never shot one before, but there was a first time for everything, right? It was better than nothing, anyway.

Surveying her pitiful arsenal, she wasn't quite sure what to do. She couldn't take on three grown men by herself, especially if she was only trying to incapacitate them. No matter how strong and proficient she was, she was not going to win against armed thugs with a four-inch pocketknife, a taser, and a flare gun. Against overwhelming odds like these, she had to push any advantage she had.

She had never taken a human life before but had long ago come to the conclusion that some people needed to die. She rubbed her throat; she knew what it was like to live in fear and be saved from the clutches of death. If needed, she would do what had to be done to protect the life of another.

Taking another peek, Lark decided to wait at the top of the rocks, hoping for either a brilliant idea or advantageous chance to show itself. Almost unconsciously, she brought the flare gun up in front of her and rested her index finger gently above the trigger.

Franklin looked much more at ease as she watched him nonchalantly glance back around for her. But when he again met her eyes, she saw fear, pain, and sorrow fill his brown ones as he glanced at the guns hanging on the sides of his kidnappers.

She tried to smile reassuringly, but he only sighed in defeat.

"I-I think I found it." He hesitated for a moment more before pulling a long silver container out of the rocks.

"Finally!" Casimer exclaimed. Stepping to the side, he casually ordered, "shoot him."

Lark reacted without thinking. While Franklin tried to scramble off the rocks to the grass, she fired the flare gun at the armed man near Franklin, then dropped it and flipped open her knife while lunging from her hiding spot onto the back of the person closest to her.

Her maneuver did manage to startle everyone, including herself. Unfortunately, the flare was wildly unpredictable. It ricocheted off her target's shoulder, leaving a sizable burn—although Lark wasn't sure if his scream was from pain or surprise—then flew toward poor Franklin.

He barely escaped the burning projectile; the flare landed right beside his foot, where it quickly fizzled out.

Oops.

Franklin jumped to the ground, looking at Lark in shock.

Sorry! she mouthed to Franklin as she dropped onto her quarry. Misjudging the distance, she didn't end up square on his back. The knife in her right hand sank into his shoulder, not his neck. But her weight and momentum did manage to knock the man down onto one knee.

Casimer yelled in rage and lunged for Franklin's silver container. Franklin swung it around to clock Casimer on the temple, which sent Casimer tumbling to hit the ground with a soft thud.

Lark tried to pull her knife back, but the serrated half got caught in her opponent's clothes. She let go of it reluctantly and focused her attention on trying to keep his hands away from the rifle still hanging at his side. Luckily, the knife must have severed some sort of nerve, rendering his trigger hand useless.

"Look out!" Franklin yelled, still clutching the container as if his life depended on it.

The man Lark shot had apparently gathered his wits. He had a small black ball in his hand, poised to throw it at them.

Before she could react, Franklin—moving with astonishing speed and strength for someone who had to be at least sixty-five—jumped. He dragged her right over the cliff edge, diving into the ocean just as a violent shock wave ripped through her body.

"What was that?" she gasped as their heads broke the surface. "A stun grenade?"

"Something like that," Franklin coughed.

They carefully climbed the rough cliff back to solid ground.

"Brilliant," Franklin scoffed with a shake of his head, studying the bodies lying prostrate on the ground. "He knocked his whole group out. That's what happens when you steal one of my inventions and use it without being instructed first." His voice had an almost comical lecturing tone, considering the circumstances. "We won't have to worry about them for a while. Now, as for you, young lady," Franklin scolded, "what on earth were you thinking? Not that we're not grateful, but—"

"We?" Lark glanced around curiously.

"Avi!" Franklin's eyes went big. "They still have him!"

"Where?" Terrifying replays of this day were probably going to haunt her later, but right now, Lark's head was surprisingly focused, even if her heart rate was through the roof. She walked over to the prone bodies. There was still work to be done. She worked her knife free and then carefully searched the unconscious men for other weapons.

"Oh no." Franklin frowned. "Our people are on their way. You have done quite enough already. I thank you, from the bottom of my heart. But I cannot, in good conscience, allow you to further endanger yourself. Give me that!" He took the grenade she'd just found.

Lark raised an eyebrow. "This guy said you had an hour before they dealt with your friend. By now, we probably have more like forty-five minutes. Will they get here in time?"

Franklin looked at his wrist grimly. Lark wondered what a thin, silver bracelet was supposed to tell him.

"I'm not sure," he finally admitted. "Probably not." He clutched the container to his chest.

"Then, it looks like you're stuck with me," Lark reasoned with a shrug.

"You have already risked too much," Franklin said.

"Look," Lark said. "I'm not sure I can save your friend. But the way I see it, without me, he dies for sure."

"Fine," Franklin sighed. "I don't have time to argue the point with you."

"Excellent. I'm Lark Bei." Lark gave him a broad smile. "Where are they holding him, and how many are there?"

Franklin sighed, then pointed to a mansion about two hundred yards up the beach. "I'm Franklin Wright. Thank you for helping us. There are six men holding Avi hostage. The rest were with me."

Lark noticed a dock with a short path that went straight to the back door.

They quickly came up with a plan—who knew all those late night strategy talks with her tactics-crazy oldest brother would come in handy so much?—as they tied up the unconscious men with their bootlaces. Just in case.

"All right," Franklin said as they got ready to part ways. "Wait until I'm in position, then you can come in."

"Roger." Lark nodded, then disappeared over the rocks again to gather her belongings.

She quickly loaded up her backpack, keeping her binoculars out, and then started up the Jet Ski.

Staying by the cove, she watched Franklin through the binoculars as he carefully picked his way toward the bored-looking figure guarding the back door.

As soon as he was safely hidden behind a sand dune about twenty yards from the back door, Lark gunned the ski, making a beeline for the dock.

"Help!" she cried, waving an arm wildly. "I need some help!"

The guard started yelling, "Go away!"

She pretended not to hear and kept the Jet Ski pointed toward the house as two more armed men came out the house's back door to join the one on the dock.

Until a spray of bullets churned the water right in front of her.

Apparently, the men was not averse to shooting at unwelcome visitors.

Hoping she was close enough, Lark heaved one of the grenades Franklin had reluctantly given her as close to them as she could, cut the engine, and dove into the water as another shock wave coursed through her body.

What are those things? she thought as she came sputtering to the surface.

Her stamina wasn't anything to sneeze at, but she was no marathon runner. She was tired, aching, and scared. She had never done anything like this before. Her brothers were the Army heroes, not her. Why did she think she could do this?

Because you're all Franklin and Avi have right now. Look at everything you've already done! Alex and Sterling might ground you forever when they find out, though, so you might as well do as much as you can now.

Smirking to herself, Lark rubbed her throat. One thing she had learned about herself: if she wasn't being choked, fear seemed to make her mind clear and jump into action, not freeze up. That was encouraging.

Still a bit dazed from the strange grenade, she clambered back onto her Jet Ski. She grunted in frustration as the engine failed to turn over. The blast must have affected it.

She was worried about Franklin. The old man said he would be in a safe spot from the blast, but there were still two more men inside to deal with. And if the guys knocked out on the dock and back porch were any indication, it wouldn't exactly be a walk in the park to subdue them.

"Come on," she coaxed the ski, turning the key one more time. The engine finally coughed back to life, but the power was next to nothing.

Lark impatiently guided the Jet Ski to the dock, grabbed her backpack and a rope from the seat, tied the vehicle to the dock, and then gingerly made her way around the unconscious men to creep in the open back door. She had kept the gun from the tussle on the beach and was now hoping the weird grenade hadn't affected its usefulness.

The mansion was huge. At least three floors. Since she didn't hear any noise and had no idea where else to start, Lark quietly searched the ground floor.

Inside the fourth room she came upon, Franklin was untying another older gentleman—Avi, Franklin had called him earlier—from a chair by the fireplace. Two prone bodies lay at their feet, blood beginning to pool beneath them.

Franklin looked up as she entered the large parlor.

"Mistress Bei! Are you all right?" Franklin, finished with his friend's restraints, stepped toward her.

"You're bleeding!" Avi said, standing and rubbing his wrists.

Lark caught her reflection in a mirror on the wall. She was still soaked and in her swimsuit, so hadn't noticed the steady stream of blood from her nose. Was it from those shockwaves?

"Wow. I look like I got worked over, don't I?" She smiled. The truth was, now that her adrenaline rush was pretty much gone, her legs were starting to feel shaky.

"Well, being exposed to the effects of the, um, grenades," Franklin shot a look at his friend as he handed her a handkerchief, "doesn't exactly bode well for one's health."

"Avi Kynaston, at your service," Avi introduced himself. "And forever in your debt. Your eyes!" he said with strange awe when he caught sight of them.

Lark was used to people doing a double take. Having two different colored eyes was unique. But he seemed especially shocked by her blue and gray eyes.

Before it got too awkward, people in black uniforms came pouring into the room, guns at the ready.

Lark brought her own back up. Where had they come from?

"Wait!" Avi's deep voice ordered. "She helped us. Mistress Bei, they are here to protect us."

"This is the backup?" Lark waited for Franklin's agreement before lowering her gun.

"While they sort out what happened, and we wait for the authorities, you are welcome to use one of our extra rooms to wash up," Avi graciously offered.

Lark realized she couldn't just walk around town like this. At the very least, she needed to get this nosebleed stopped. "Thank you."

"Avi, if you could show Mistress Bei to the bathroom, I'll make sure everyone else is taken care of properly," Franklin said.

CHAPTER 7

"**M**y job is head of the royal guard." Harold's voice brought Lark back to the present. Or future, depending on how one looked at it. "Protecting King Avi and Franklin is ultimately my responsibility. I wasn't there that day, and several of the Wysteria Corps had been bribed by Casimer to become traitors. If it weren't for you..." Harold cleared his throat. "The kingdom of Lothar owes you a debt she can never repay."

Lark shook her head. "I just happened to be the person there at the right time. Or maybe the wrong time." She chuckled.

"I've always wondered what possessed you to jump into the fray instead of running away," Harold said.

They were still sitting on the comfortable chairs in the front of the vacation bus, but the tiger cub had worked her way behind Lark's back to play with her long ponytail.

"I'm an idiot?" Lark laughed at Harold's frown, then shrugged. "Every martial art teacher I had said that in an emergency, you fall to the level of your training." She brought the pair of dog tags out from her shirt to look lovingly at them. "Whether my brothers meant to or not, they taught me to think through a situation, figure out the options. And to protect others. I guess I fell to the level of my training."

She looked up to see Harold and Conan studying her. She felt like Conan had been testing her before, or maybe expecting something from her. But his expression was much softer now.

She lowered her gaze.

"What did you do after saving them?" Conan finally asked.

"As my Jet Ski was being fixed, they treated me to a scrumptious homemade meal." Lark's mouth watered just thinking about it. "When I finally checked the clock, I realized I was going to be late for an appointment that had taken months to set up. I vaguely recall yelling apologies as I ran out of there like I was on fire." She laughed. "I really enjoyed talking with Mr. Franklin and Avi over the next couple of weeks. My brothers, Alex and Sterling, wanted to meet them after hearing the story. Sterling usually likes everyone he meets, so it was no surprise they got along great. But even stoic Alex warmed up to them. We sent them some letters once we got to our new duty station, but we never heard from them again. What happened?"

"Time travel is pretty new," Harold said. "We're still figuring out the rules and idiosyncrasies. It's taken us four years to find you again."

"Four years?" Lark furrowed her brow. "It's been three years for me."

Harold nodded. "The perks of time travel. The harder part of time travel is the fact that you need a certain set of circumstances for a trip—ingredients, if you will. The farther away the destination, the more ingredients you need. And unfortunately, those tend to move around."

"Move around?" For some reason, an image of a frog jumping all over, slipping through grasping fingers, popped in her head. While it was entertaining, it didn't make Harold's explanation any clearer.

Harold grimaced. "Sorry, I'm not the most knowledge-able about this. My other son, Joshua, will be able to answer your questions more thoroughly. But here's the short version. Time travel is still an imprecise science. Trying to find someone two thousand years in the past, on a differ-ent planet no less, was not an easy task. We were finally reasonably sure we had found a path to you, so we began plotting out this route. About a week ago, Doctor Franklin was on his way to meet us from a diplomatic meeting in a neighboring country when he was attacked. Investigations are currently underway, but there were no indications the attackers knew he was trying to come for you. Right now, we're assuming it was just an attempt to kidnap him gone wrong. He is—was—a very prominent man here. Unfortu-nately, he was injured, as you know. He managed to tell us what happened and found the closest place he could use for a time jump. We followed the signal he sent us."

"Wait," Lark shook her head. "You said he was attacked a week ago?"

Harold nodded. "It took us several days to get every-thing we needed to the most sustainable jump point. If we have a beacon, like the one Franklin sent us, we can easily do a round trip to and from the signal, as long as there are enough particles to sustain the jump."

"Without that signal, though," Conan chimed in, "it's much harder getting to a specific time or place so far away. Long story short, you lost touch with King Avi and Doctor Franklin in the past because they couldn't get back. They never got your letters."

"It's kind of a relief to know they weren't ignoring us," Lark said. She and her brothers didn't often give overtures of friendship. "We were sad they didn't stay in touch. I remember thinking it would be really fun to have a grand-father like them."

She fiddled with the dog tags again. Harold shifted his gaze uncomfortably. Thinking he was wondering about the dog tags, Lark held them up.

"My brothers'. They gave me copies as a birthday pres-ent a few years before...before I lost them." Her voice got a little hoarse at the end, trying to hold back sudden tears. Two years since the gut-wrenching notification. Every time she remembered it, was still like a knife in the heart. Not wanting to dwell on it, Lark plastered a smile on her face. "Is anyone else hungry?"

Harold looked like he wanted to say something else, but he nodded and said, "This isn't a bad spot to break for an early dinner. We'll make camp here tonight, then send the vacation bus back in the morning."

"Send the bus where in the morning?" Lark followed Conan out into the fresh afternoon sunshine.

A couple of their companions climbed into the vacated bus, making use of the mini kitchen to prepare a large dinner. Altogether, their company numbered twenty. Everyone but Conan, Harold, and Lark had been following the bus on their own hoverbikes, some pulling small storage containers behind.

"Your arrival needs to stay secret for now," Conan answered. "Airplanes and sky trams are too public. Hoverbike is going to be the fastest way to get over these mountains and back to our capital, Vusal."

"Really?" Lark looked at the closest bike curiously, excited to try one herself.

"Hovercraft run off of Hewa energy, usually with enough juice to last about two or three days without recharging. But the larger the craft, the longer it takes to recharge if it's not near a Hewa battery. We'd have to sit still for twelve hours every couple of days if we kept the vacation bus. The bikes will recharge enough each night for us to get home within a week."

Lark nodded, pretending she understood anything Conan was saying.

I'm already getting a headache with all the new things I have to learn.

"Lark!" Shamira's voice called.

Lark watched her trot up from where she had been talking with Harold, a broad grin lighting up her face.

"There's something just through the trees I think you'll like," Sharmia said. "The commander general said we could take you while we wait for food." She motioned to Conan.

Curious, Lark shifted the tiger cub to a more comfortable position in her arms. "All right, show the way."

A light breeze rustled the trees as the trio set out, wrapping a refreshing, clean scent around them. Was that a waterfall she heard in the distance? When they pushed their way through a thick line of bushes, Lark found herself in a meadow.

"Are these real?" she whispered.

Instead of the wide range of soft pastels she was used to seeing, these wildflowers were something...otherworldly. Sparkling in the sunlight, the flowers looked closer to gems. Blossoms of every shape and size looked like they were made of rubies, emeralds, sapphires, topaz, pearls... Lark ran out of jewels she knew to compare them to. Even the greenery had a metallic sheen to it one couldn't find on Earth. Was this why everything seemed odd to her eyes?

Lark let the tiger down to frolic, allowing herself to sink to her knees. She reached out a hesitant hand to touch a metallic purple flower, half expecting to feel cool, hard stone as opposed to the velvety softness that greeted her fingers. She looked up at her companions, who were watching her with amusement.

"Look a little different than you're used to?" Conan teased.

"Is this normal here?" Lark asked.

"On Evren, yes." Shamira nodded. "Other planets have different dominant colors."

"Dominant colors?" Lark asked.

"Each terraformed planet's makeup influences colors a little differently," Conan said. "Evren's dominant chemicals and minerals make jewel and metallic tones the most common here. Atlantis has more pastels, and Mars has earthy, coppery tones."

"Mars? People are really living on Mars?" Lark squeaked excitedly.

I really shouldn't be surprised by anything anymore. If I'm standing on a different planet two thousand years in the future, of course Mars would be an obvious choice.

"Oh yes." Lark barely heard Shamira. "There are four inhabited planets. Earth is still alive and kicking, although it was questionable for a while there. Then Atlantis, Mars, and Evren were terraformed."

"I wish Alex and Sterling could be here with me. Their minds would be blown," Lark whispered, touching the dog tags under her shirt.

She inhaled sharply when an idea struck.

Time travel! Why didn't I think of this before? If there's a chance I could save my brothers...but, I've got to know more. There's too much that could go wrong. What was the name of Harold's son...

"Joshua?" Lark accidentally said out loud.

Conan glanced over. "Josh? My brother?"

"Brother?" Lark's eyes widened. "The time travel guy?"

"Yeah. Joshua Cynbel. One of those annoyingly brilliant geniuses," Conan said in a playful tone. Lark could hear the pride in his voice.

"So you and Harold...?" Lark wasn't sure why this was so difficult to grasp.

"Yep." Conan grinned. "Mr. Salt and Pepper is my dad."

Lark blushed furiously. "Am I ever going to live that down?" she groaned.

"Probably not," Conan laughed.

She hadn't paid attention before, but Lark could see similar facial structure between father and son. Strong jaw, long nose. Instead of his father's hazel eyes, Conan's were blue. Although now that she really looked at them, they also had pretty green specks.

"Josh could have turned his hand to anything," Conan said, interrupting Lark's thoughts about pretty blue eyes. "But he practically breathes formulas and equations.

Director Franklin discovered the time travel particles and invented the bio-bots, but Joshua was key in their development."

Lark perked up at this. Maybe she wouldn't be stumbling blindly when it came to understanding the new her.

And it sounds like he should have all the answers I need about time travel, as well! For a chance to save Alex and Sterling, I would accept any job—even inheriting a planet 2,000 years in the future.

Conan looked down at his silver bracelet. When he pressed something on it, a small black holographic box about half the size of his hand appeared above his wrist. When Conan announced dinner was ready, Lark realized the black box must have been a form of texting.

Lark glanced at her own empty wrist, remembering she was the only one in their group without a matching bracelet. It must be a team or unit marking. It had been a long time since she had felt part of a group.

Everyone needed friends and allies. Holding these guys at arm's length would be stupid.

She snuck glances at Shamira and Conan as they helped her chase the white tiger cub around the meadow. She was a little out of practice in the making friends department, but Conan had definitely warmed up to her since their first meeting. Shamira seemed like a fun, energetic young woman. Both looked near her age.

Instead of rescuing her brothers and staying on Earth, maybe, just maybe, she could create a safe home for her family here, in the future. And if being a Kynaston gave them that security, then so be it.

CHAPTER 8

When Lark, Conan and Shamira finally caught the cub, she allowed Shamira to carry her back to camp. As they approached Harold, who was waiting for them by the vacation bus door, Shamira turned to Lark. "Are you going to name her?" She nodded to the cub purring in her arms.

Lark rubbed her ear. The purring seemed awfully loud for a tiny little cub. But then again, she had grown up with a dog, not cats.

"It might make it harder when I have to let her go, but yes," Lark said sadly.

"You won't have to part with her," Conan promised.

"You seem awfully sure about that." Lark raised an eyebrow as they joined the line for a food-laden table next to the bus.

"First, let me explain a bit about the forming of our worlds. The terraforming process of a planet takes time,"

Conan started. "When a planet has been deemed a good candidate, the machines that help create an atmosphere are brought down." He held up his hands. "Before you ask a bunch of questions, I'm not a scientist. But thanks to Josh, I know a little bit. Only a little bit."

Lark nodded, even more eager to meet this third member of the Cynbel family.

"Once the atmosphere is established, it becomes self-sustaining. But each planet has a different makeup, resulting in different plants and colors based on the core materials and chemicals."

Lark smiled, thinking about the jeweled meadow they had just come from. She took the cub from Shamira and deposited the cub on her shoulders so all their hands were free to load their plates with food.

"In an attempt to make the terraformed planets safer for the human occupants, the predatory animals that were introduced to the new ecosystems were given some cocktail of drugs targeting their brains so they wouldn't be as prone to attack humans. Some species seemed to eventually grow out of it, while others became noticeably easier to domesticate. Nobody knows the exact reason, but felines didn't seem to do well on terraformed planets."

Concerned, Lark scratched the cub's ears, not sure if she was trying to soothe herself or the tiger. She followed Conan and Shamira to sit in the shade of a nearby tree.

"The entire species are considered endangered. Any cats, especially the large breeds, found in nature are protected by all governments. I'm not sure why, perhaps because they're the biggest breed of cat, but starting from a long time ago the tiger was widely viewed as a symbol of power. Royal families and governments reserved the sole right to keep tigers as pets, on the condition the tigers themselves accepted them. Most kept their wild instincts, but very rarely there will be a tiger with a disposition closer to a house cat. But it's uncommon even catching a glimpse of a tiger, much less forming a bond with one. Anyone in power that could prove a bond would practically have all four planets salivating over them. It's viewed more as a status symbol nowadays, but legend has it that anyone with a Tiger Bond was more powerful and special, their influence rippling across the galaxies."

"Personally, I think it's just because people *give* those with a Tiger Bond more power and influence since they seem special." Shamira shrugged.

"But I'm nobody." Lark frowned, wanting to cry. "There's no way I could keep her."

When Lark had pulled the crying cub out from under the rock, they had seemed to instinctively reach out to each other. For the cub, it was probably just the real need for a replacement of the mother she was still dependent on. But now that Lark had responded to that need, she didn't want to give it up.

"No one will question your right to keep her." Lark jumped from Harold's unexpected voice coming behind her.

"Why?" Lark began to feel a little suspicious. "You said..." She stood and glanced around at the uncomfortable faces of her companions.

"King Avi is the ruler of this land, Lothar," Harold said in an infuriatingly calm voice. "You made quite an impression on him. When he got back from that trip, he adopted you and your brothers, and named you heir to his throne."

Lark blinked. "Excuse me?"

She looked at everyone waiting for her response, not sure if she was looking for confirmation on Harold's statement or not.

"Why would he do that? He only knew us for a couple weeks, then disappeared, never contacting us again," Lark said. She would rather die right now than admit to the tiny part of her that warmed for no good reason at the thought Avi wouldn't have tried to separate her family. As wrong as bringing her whole family to the future might have been, it seemed like he would have accepted all of them.

Harold shrugged. "That's something you'll need to ask His Majesty yourself."

"How did he even adopt us? We're all adults," said Lark.

"What the king wants, the king gets," Harold said, almost apologetically.

Lark raised an eyebrow. There had to be more to it than that.

"He was awfully insistent about you." Conan seemed to study her intently. "But he wouldn't tell anyone why."

"I would imagine he will tell you when we get home," Harold said, although Lark didn't think he sounded so sure about that.

Lark wanted to rub her temples to alleviate the headache she suddenly found she had. Seeming to sense something was wrong, the cub meowed and pawed at her chin. Lark decided to leave the endless questions swimming in her head for Avi. The people here either didn't have the answers, or they were going to give their king a chance to explain everything himself.

"So, not only did I somehow end up with weird little organisms that changed my very genetic makeup, but brothers and I have apparently been adopted by some king, old enough to be my grandfather, from a different planet, two thousand years in the future. Did I get that right?" Lark didn't bother keeping the sarcasm out of her voice. "And the person who decided these things were okay without my consent also happens to be said king."

Harold winced. "Looks like you have a lot to talk about."

"I'm so excited," Lark deadpanned.

Harold cleared his throat before giving her a small bow and escaping the awkwardness.

Lark watched him walk away, then turned toward her lunch companions, who seemed like they wanted to be anywhere but there.

"So." Lark paused, not sure what to do. "How do you all fit into the picture? Are you my bodyguards?"

To her surprise, Conan nodded. "The royal guards are known as the Wysteria Corps. But we, your own personal squad, are called the Spur Corps."

A painful thought occurred to her. "Are there rules about us being friends?"

Shamira shook her head. "There aren't any set rules forbidding it, although it really depends on the person."

"Dad and King Avi are actually very good friends," Conan said. "The king always treated my brother and me like his grandkids."

"I'm glad," Lark said softly before taking a large bite of pink-colored mashed potatoes. "Wow, this is delicious!" They were so creamy, and perfectly seasoned. It seemed like food was still excellent in the future.

"Enjoy it, because this and tomorrow's breakfast will be the last meals with real food until we get to Vusal," Shamira warned.

Hmm. Maybe I spoke too soon.

"What do you mean 'real food?'" Lark asked.

"We took advantage of the vacation bus kitchen these first few days," Conan said. "But starting tomorrow, we will just have replacement rations."

Lark wrinkled her nose. She had no idea what those were, but they sounded nasty. Before anyone could tell her differently, the cub made a play for the steaming slab of meat on her plate.

"Whoa, little girl!" Lark laughed, pulling her away from the food. "I'm not sure what your stomach can handle right now."

Shamira laughed. "She really is adorable! When she's curled up, she looks like a big, fluffy, black and white snowball."

"Snowball!" Lark and Shamira gasped at the same time.

"Snowball what?" Conan looked up from his plate.

"I think we just found her name." Lark smiled.

After dinner, Lark decided to go to sleep and rest. It was her last chance to use the comfortable bed, so she might as well make the most of it. Besides, she was tired. Tomorrow was soon enough to learn more about this strange new world.

"I'll join you in a minute, girl." Lark smiled as Snowball—Snowy for short—made herself at home on the soft bed. "I've got to get changed."

As she pulled out those silky pajamas from before, Lark pondered about her skin. It still felt stretched just a little too tight. Flexing her hands a few times, she studied her arms. They looked normal, but maybe they felt a little hard? Difficult to tell, not having a gauge of her new strength.

Hmm. Lark fingered her pocketknife. *What would it hurt? I heal pretty fast now, even if the blade does cut.* Glancing at the door to be sure no one was spying on her, Lark pressed the blade to the back of her arm. And pressed. *Nothing? Wow.* Lark narrowed her eyes, remembering her broken arm earlier. *Pretty tough on the outside, but not quite as indestructible from the inside?*

Wondering how much this hardened skin covered, Lark first pinched her legs and stomach before trying the knife on those areas. Not even a dent. Wanting to test her back, she slipped the knife in her pocket and called for Shamira.

"Did you happen to pack a mirror?" Lark asked when Shamira came in.

"Oh, I'm sure there was one. Let me see." Shamira dropped to her knees and started rummaging through a chest she pulled out from under the bed. "Here it is!"

"Thank you," Lark said, taking the small mirror. She glanced at her reflection, and nearly dropped the mirror from shock. "What?"

"What's that matter?" Shamira leaped to her feet.

Lark turned to her new friend and pointed at her own face. "What color are my eyes?"

"Oh, they're beautiful! I've been wanting to comment about them all day. A deep sapphire blue and dark metallic silver. We were told you had blue and gray eyes, but not that they looked like jewels!"

"That's because they didn't! Not two days ago! Or two thousand years ago. Whatever."

Lark spun back to the mirror. Why this little detail threatened to overcome her, she wasn't sure. But looking at those unfamiliar eyes only reinforced how much had changed over the last two days. She might know every thought and feeling of the reflection in front of her, but she no longer *knew* the woman looking back at her.

Must everything about my brothers be taken away from me?

"I would like to be alone." Lark's voice was rough with emotion.

"Are you sure?" Shamira asked.

Lark nodded sharply, not willing to show the tears pooling in those strange, foreign eyes. And to think she had envied the jewel tone of Shamira's emerald orbs. She heard Shamira gently close the door behind her.

Lark took one more look at the interloper in the mirror. Three days ago, she had been wrapping up her part-time job, getting ready for premed classes. Today, she was expected to rule and protect a kingdom she hadn't even known existed.

There was no going back to her past life. She knew that. Not with a tiger and superpowers. And she really was willing to make the most of what she had. She would try to learn her place here and figure out how to use her new resources for her family. But for now, just for now...

She curled up on the bed, clutching her dog tags, with the comforting warmth of Snowy against her chest, and let the tears flow.

CHAPTER 9

"**D**o we have a problem, Talbot?"

Casimer shivered, as he did every time the smooth, sultry voice pronounced his name. She somehow made it sound poisonous.

"Not at all. Simply a delay."

Casimer hated the fact he needed her help. If he wasn't careful, she would be the death of him, not his trump card in regaining his rightful place. He would put off admitting to the loss of Franklin for as long as he could. Maybe he could come up with something that would soothe her rage.

There was a long, suffocating pause before the line went dead.

Steele Jones poured over his holographic map with serious, gray eyes, zooming in on the map to make note of where the rivers were. There had been reported sightings of Wysteria Corps members in a couple of the closest cities. While it wasn't totally unheard of to see the royal guard throughout the kingdom, it wasn't common to see high level commanders like the Cynbels away from the royal family.

Steele and Beck had gone over likely land routes. Steele had sent his scouts out. Now all he could do was wait. At least this assignment was in a nice spot. Steele loved being outdoors.

After Earth was nearly destroyed due to deforestation, the preservation of nature was highly valued on all planets. It was a high priority for all the countries on Evren, but Lothar was by far the largest. From Lothar's foundation, vast expanses of reserves had been set up throughout the land, which was sparsely populated. It was also completely legal for people to camp and explore these reserves, as long as they respected the land.

Steele had taken advantage of one such reserve to set up his temporary headquarters in a network of natural caves in a high mountain range. He liked it here. If Casimer ever gave them a vacation, and he would convince Beck to leave his side; this would be an ideal place to relax.

The familiar feeling of loathing Steele always got while thinking of Casimer settled in the pit of his stomach like a spiky stone. Steele frowned, thinking about the way Beck respected and idolized the disinherited former prince. In Steele's opinion, Casimer was entitled and selfish. Any gratitude and sense of debt for saving their lives had long since disappeared. But Beck insisted on staying with Casimer and championing his cause.

Thanks to that, Casimer preferred to keep the loyal, tactically brilliant Beck near his side and send the versatile, quick-thinking Steele out on endless errands across the planet.

Steele groaned as the pain which normally stayed a low ache behind his eyes expand to his entire skull. The tall man sat down wearily, pinching the bridge of his sharp, angled nose, then rubbed his temples in an attempt to alleviate the throbbing in his head.

He would have to check in with Casimer soon, but he had begun postponing it as long as he could. Some days it seemed like he could go a bit longer before his head started splitting from the pain, which gave him enough hope to continue his little inward rebellion.

Steele was determined to break Beck from Casimer's hold. One day, they would both be free.

But until then, he should probably call Casimer and get this over with.

Lark made sure all traces of tears were gone before venturing out of the vacation bus for breakfast the next morning. She studied her eyes in the mirror just long enough to assure herself they weren't red or puffy, then stuffed it deep into the chest Shamira had found it in.

As she reached for the bedroom door, she paused. There was some...thing...on the other side.

How would I know that?

She couldn't bring herself to turn the handle. There was some sort of energy in the bus. Maybe. Whatever was there was giving her a ticklish feeling. She had to stifle a squeak of surprise when someone knocked on her door.

Snowy rubbed her body against Lark's foot.

"Princess Larkspur?" Shamira's voice said before another knock.

Lark cleared her throat and opened the door. "Just Lark is fine."

Shamira smiled at her. "I came to teach you about clothes."

I need to be taught how to get dressed? Lark looked down at her old cargo pants, boots, and faded purple t-shirt. *Well, it would be nice to wear clean clothes.*

"Most clothes are made of nano-cloth now," Shamira said, grabbing a small, silky bag from that blasted chest.

Lark watched curiously as Shamira emptied out buttons, snaps, and zippers of all different shapes, colors, and sizes into her palm.

"So." Shamira grinned at Lark with a twinkle in her eye. "What would you like to wear?"

Lark looked at the assembly of buttons Shamira was showing her with confusion.

What am I supposed to do with a button?

"Do you want pants? A jacket? What color?" Shamira asked as she held each button over her Spur corps bracelet.

"Uh, cargo pants would be great. I like pockets," Lark said slowly, still unsure what Shamira was doing. "The springs here seem to be pretty mild, so I don't think I need a jacket. Just as long as the clothes are comfortable and I can move easily, I'm good. I don't really care what color, either."

Shamira nodded, picked a blue button about the size of a dime, then looked expectantly at Lark. "Take off all your clothes."

"Excuse me?" Lark blinked.

"This will dress you. They'll even take care of your undergarments, but I'll understand if you'd rather keep those for now. There is comfort in familiarity." Shamira smiled.

Lark looked at Snowy sitting on the bed playing with the bag of buttons, not sure if it was a plea for help. Whether it was or not, Snowy just cocked her head cutely and blinked her blue eyes at Lark.

Lark sighed, then slowly stripped.

Shamira twisted the top half of the button to the right twice, then to the left once.

"Here." She placed the button in Lark's hand. "This might feel a little weird the first time."

"What's going to feel weird?" Lark held her hand out, looking at the button suspiciously. Then she nearly jumped out of her skin when something that resembled royal blue liquid leaked from the button. It moved up her forearm, wrapped around her bicep, then elongated. There was a short sleeve. Now half her torso was covered in a royal blue material. Once the loose, flowing shirt was done, black pants started to materialize over her legs.

Even after it was done, Lark stood frozen for some time.

"You were right. That was weird," she finally said.

Shamira stifled a giggle. "You'll get used to it. There are some great advantages to nano-clothes." They made their way to the front of the bus, where she started cooking a scrumptious breakfast. "You can store multiple outfits on one object. Most average two to three, but the more expensive ones can store more, and have different designs programmed in."

Lark sat at the small table, feeding Snowy some warmed milk in her lap. Lark fingered her left sleeve, feeling the material between her fingers, then ran her hand down the pants.

"Sure feels like the clothes I'm used to," she said with a little awe.

"Good!" Shamira brought over two plates filled with steaming seasoned eggs, crispy bacon, and mouthwatering fruit. "I'm glad there's a little something that feels like your old home."

Old home. I don't really have a new home yet, though.

Deciding not to dwell on that thought, Lark dug in.

"This is so good!" She barely remembered to finish swallowing before praising the simple, but delicious breakfast. "I'm so happy there's still real food in the future."

Shamira laughed. "New dishes have been invented, I'm sure. But food basics haven't changed much that I'm aware of."

"Well, I'm just glad no one has come up with printed food or something."

Shamira wrinkled her nose. "Something like that was tried, maybe five hundred years ago? But it didn't take. No one has been able to replicate the pure taste of real food."

Lark nodded firmly as she inhaled the last of her breakfast.

"Of course, we have things like replacement rations. But they're only used when needed. All the nutrients of a full meal can be had in one little rectangle of powdery nastiness." Shamira made a disgusted face.

"Sounds gross." Lark grimaced.

"It is."

The front door opened, and one of the men entered the vacation bus. Lark remembered meeting him during introductions to everyone yesterday, but she couldn't recall his name.

"Colonel, your highness." He gave a slight bow.

For a second, Lark forgot she was "your highness."

"Something has happened; what, I'm not sure," he said. "I have to take the bus back now, and you all need to get ready to head out. I'll take the sky tram back home."

Shamira stood and clapped him on the shoulder. "Thank you. Stay safe. We'll see you in a week or two."

Shamira went outside while Lark scrambled up, made sure all her belongings were stuffed in her backpack, then mumbled a thank you and goodbye to the man sitting patiently in the bus's driver seat.

Stepping outside, Lark was greeted with a tense hustle and bustle. People whispered in strained tones. Last night's camp was being packed away quickly, a worried air hanging over everything.

Lark spotted Harold and Conan huddled together, a holographic map open between them. Colored pixels that seemed to come from Harold's silver bracelet created a map with rivers, mountains, and the names of all the features. There was something about the electric currents making up the hologram that pulled Lark. It wasn't as strong as the fire, but it was enough that she started walking toward it, a strange buzz under her skin.

Hearing her footsteps, Harold and Conan turned serious faces toward her, temporarily overriding the disturbing energy connection.

"Did something happen?" she asked.

"It's possible Franklin's attackers might have realized he was bringing the bio-bots to the person they were programmed to," Harold said. "It was just confirmed the country he was in, Crofton, was behind the attack. While we don't know if he was behind it, they do have ties to Casimer Talbot. Their prime minister is an old school chum of Casimer's. He shouldn't know your identity, and there's no reason for them to know about our plan, but we're going to err on the side of caution. We'll split into two groups. About half of us are taking you over the mountain; the others will take the longer path around the base."

Lark felt a flutter in her stomach, but couldn't decide if it was anticipation, excitement, nerves, or outright fear. Maybe a bit of everything.

Harold turned to her, a look of sheepish annoyance on his face.

"Did I do something?" Lark furrowed her brow.

Harold shook his head, face softening. "No, I'm angry at myself. I forgot to give you this." He held up a silver bracelet that nearly matched Franklin and Avi's. The shiny silver was engraved with the wisteria tree and tiger, but it had a larkspur flower added beneath the tree trunk.

"The Spur Corps have the flower added." The realization brought a smile to Lark's lips.

Harold nodded. "These have a tracking beacon to be used in case of emergencies. Well, there's more to it than that, but we'll go over everything they do later. For now, let's program your fingerprint so you can activate the beacon, if needed."

Lark reached out for the bracelet. But when Harold dropped it into her eager hands, there was a spark. The tree engraving flashed purple for a second, then a small trail of smoke puffed and dissolved.

She looked at Harold with wide eyes.

"Are you okay?" He gingerly took the bracelet back to inspect it.

"I'm fine, I think." Lark studied her hands briefly. "I feel a little buzzy, full of energy."

Harold knit his eyebrows together. "I don't know exactly how the bio-bots work, but I do remember Franklin and Joshua talking about them holding energy." It sounded more like a question than a statement.

"Is that dangerous?" Lark froze. The last thing she wanted was to electrocute her whole team of bodyguards.

Harold looked apologetic. "Franklin was supposed to be with us to help explain things."

"Well, I'm sure no one will die, right?" Lark was only half joking.

Harold paused awkwardly. "I'll have Conan show you how to operate a hoverbike." He turned.

"Actually, could I keep the bracelet?"

"If you wish." Harold looked puzzled but handed it over. "I'll make sure it gets fixed when we get home."

Lark watched him walk away, a tiny smile flirting with her lips. Even if the electrical component of the bracelet was broken, it still marked her as part of the group. Still learning about her place in this new world, but not alone anymore. She had a team, and the evidence was sitting on her wrist.

CHAPTER 10

Driving a hoverbike ended up being way easier than Lark thought it would be. She barely used a bicycle growing up and hadn't even sat on a motorcycle before. Thankfully, the hover mechanism kept these bikes standing, so riding wasn't the balancing act Lark expected.

In fact, it was even better than a convertible since they were so much more maneuverable. Her biggest worry was Snowy. There weren't compartments or saddle bags on the side of her bike, so the cub sat enthroned in Lark's backpack. Lark had moved it to her front so she was able to keep an eye on the furry face that occasionally stuck her nose out into the racing wind.

After the incident with her bracelet, the buzzing electricity Lark had felt stayed with her. Not only that, but by the time they stopped to make camp for the night, she realized something else. She was now hyperaware and sensitive to energy sources, even beginning to tell when they were close by.

Lark was disappointed she couldn't tell Shamira about this discovery, since she was in the other group going the long way around the mountain.

I wish I could ask for her help experimenting with this new...development.

With their heated sleeping bags and replacement rations, there was no need to build a fire for either cooking or warmth. But one was still graciously made when Lark asked. She tried not to stare as the kindling took and grew into a blaze. She really did. But the buzz, tickle, and pull grew with the flames.

Not at all sure what to do about it, she ended up just ogling the fire until a shake of her shoulder snapped her out of it. She turned to see Conan giving her a strange look—as if he was caught between feeling amused and frustrated about gaining such a weird boss.

"Are you all right?" Conan asked.

"Fine." Lark cleared her throat, embarrassed.

She turned back to the fire, then glanced at her hand, which was beginning to tingle even more.

Hmm. Well, nothing ventured, nothing gained! Let's see what I can do.

ξξξ

Conan's heart skipped a beat when his confusing charge stuck her hand in the fire with no warning.

"What in heaven's name are you thinking?" he nearly yelled, snatching her arm back.

They both stared at her unscathed hand, though Lark seemed much calmer than he was. He probably should have known she would be fine, since she ingested a dangerous amount of radiation without breaking a sweat, but a heads-up would have been nice.

They were going to have to start communicating better, or working together was going to be difficult.

Lark looked back and forth between her hand and the fire. "If I can store energy, there's got to be a way to use it, right?"

Conan's jaw dropped. "You're an Elemental Wielder?"

That would explain a lot! But why the heck wouldn't I be told? He had to push away a wave of anger.

"A what?" Lark finally looked away from the fire to fix him with a questioning look.

"Elemental Wielder," Conan answered. "Someone who can manipulate an element."

"Like, magic?" Lark asked, excitement and curiosity lacing her voice.

Conan shook his head. "It's called arcane science. Josh likes to say everything is science. Some of it is just currently unexplained or unexplored."

"So, it's sciencey magic?" Lark furrowed her brow.

Sighing, Conan decided to let Josh handle this one. "Sure. Sciencey magic."

"So, how do I learn it?" Lark's eyes shone.

Conan shook his head. "I have no idea. As far as we know, humans have always had the ability, but no one actually uses it."

"Why? Is it too dangerous?" Lark sounded disappointed.

"No, it's useless." Conan shrugged. "It takes so much energy to manipulate whatever your element is, you'd die long before it would be helpful. I have an affinity for air—"

"You can manipulate air?" Lark's look of admiration made him not want to admit the next part.

"Well, yes. But like I said, it's useless. Just moving a tiny puff of air knocks me out cold for over an hour. I gave up trying to do anything with it a long time ago."

Lark looked disappointed.

Conan smiled softly. "I think the bio-bots give you a chance to actually do something with it, though."

Lark brightened again. "What is my element? Fire?"

"That would be my guess."

Lark looked thoughtfully behind them where other members of their group were preparing for bed, then back to the fire. Conan was curious what she was thinking, but decided not to push.

"I'll leave you to play with the fire. Just don't forget to sleep at some point," he said.

Lark absentmindedly nodded as Conan went to get some shut-eye.

"If we find ourselves under attack, the four of us will ride down this hill and split up if we're followed." Conan looked at two of his men and Lark as they stood at the crest of a steep slope. "Hopefully, this will give at least Lark enough of a head start to meet up with help."

They were breaking for lunch the second day after splitting into two groups. Behind them was a grassy clearing, about fifty yards in expanse. On the far side stood a large pile of boulders. Two guards stood watch on top of the stones. Near the base, someone was setting up a small campfire.

"Why do I have to leave everyone behind?" Lark protested. "I don't want to abandon you all. I can't ask you to risk your lives for me if I'm not willing to face the same risk."

"While the sentiment is appreciated, your highness," Harold said as she joined them, "you are not only our priority, but you could also very well pose a threat yourself. Without a handle on your new abilities, you could end up hurting rather than helping us."

Harold glanced meaningfully at the fire. Lark snorted indignantly, but apparently couldn't refute Harold's warning.

"Could you watch Snowy for a bit?" she asked Conan.

"Sure." Conan held the cub, who squirmed in his arms before finally giving a grunt and settling down.

As if to prove her worth, Lark strode toward the fire.

Conan sighed. Poor Lark. He still had his reservations about this near-stranger, but it couldn't be easy—landing into an intense new job, coming to terms with abilities even this time still thought of as fantasy, and then being told you couldn't use them properly.

After that first spark with her bracelet, which seemed to jumpstart something in her, she hadn't overloaded anything else, but she was avoiding anything electrical, just to be on the safe side.

He looked forward to showing her VPhones. Considering how excited she was about the holographic capabilities of their bracelets, her eyes were going to shine when she knew vid-calls and texts were now holograms. You could still do a voice call, known as vo-calls, but he guessed she was going to play with the vid-calls for a while.

Conan made a detour to get some water for Snowy before settling himself and the cub next to Lark, who was sticking her hand in and out of the fire.

In the beginning, she just absorbed the flames. Now she could pull them to her hand from a small distance. So far, she was only holding the flames in the palm of her hand—where they turned a pretty purple color—or absorbing them into her body. But she was determined to find out if she could manipulate them in some way.

"What does it feel like?" Conan asked.

The original plan was to bring Lark to the planet much closer to home. They had prepared areas on the palace grounds to help safely develop the bio-bots enhancements. The attack on Franklin was causing a lot of headaches, including the mysterious heir to Lothar's throne blindly stumbling upon new abilities.

"A little warm." Lark's eyes sparkled mischievously.

Conan rolled his eyes.

"Sometimes it tickles a little," Lark said more seriously. "I can keep myself from absorbing all the flames into me. Mostly. Beyond that, I'm not really sure what I'm doing."

"You've been working hard at this, but it *has* only been two days," Conan reminded her. The forerunner usually had the hardest time learning the ins and outs of something new.

"True," Lark agreed reluctantly.

"The next generation of bio-bots probably won't be the exact same, but it will still be helpful having your experiences to refer back to."

Lark nodded, still staring into the fire. Then she jerked her gaze toward him. "Wait, what do you mean?"

"You were never meant to be the only one with bio-bots. With your help, Joshua might be able to make a slightly different version, and we can still join you in the Shield Unit."

"We?"

"You're the leader of the Shield Unit. Who better to lead than your own Spur Corps?" Conan smirked. "We're already a force dedicated to you. It made sense to keep it all in the family."

"I like it." Lark gave a small smile. "Although I'm still unsure about why you're creating the Shield Unit."

"The bio-bots were originally invented because we had been threatened with invasion by an enemy bent on war and savagery," Conan said. "We have a strong military, but Evren has been largely peaceful ever since its foundation. The bio-bots were to help give us an edge. While that particular instance was smoothed over diplomatically, there are those of us who want to be ready in case something like that happens again, so Franklin continued with the bio-bots' creation."

"I'm supposed to be responsible for something like that?" Lark said so softly, Conan wasn't sure he was supposed to hear it.

He saw maybe not outright fear, but there was a wary uncertainty in Lark's expression before she refocused on the purple ball of fire in her palm. Conan hadn't been in favor of a stranger from the past becoming heir, but he had seen leadership potential in Lark since meeting her. Grandpa Avi seemed so confident in her abilities that he was willing to give her a chance.

Snowy surprised Conan by jumping from his lap, wanting to paw at the flames in Lark's hand.

"You, little girl, are not fireproof," Conan chided Snowy, pulling her away.

He eventually distracted her with a long stick. Soon, she was happily shredding the wood at his feet, and he could watch Lark again.

Conan smiled, admiring how the firelight reflected in the jewel tones of Lark's eyes. The natural spectrum of eye and hair color had widened over the last two thousand years. Lark's new, darker eye colors weren't unnatural here, but having complete heterochromia was still rare.

Realizing he was still staring at Lark, Conan gave himself a mental shake. What was he doing again? Oh, right, Snowy. He cleared his throat and pat the cub to distract himself from Lark's eyes.

"Conan, look!" Lark practically squealed.

He peered up to watch Lark gently push her palm forward. The purple flame floated from her hand to dissolve back into the campfire.

"Whoa," he breathed.

Eyes shining, Lark reached into the blaze to scoop out another handful of flame.

"Commander general!" The yell from one of the sentries on the rock above them startled both Conan and Larkspur.

But what surprised them more was the thin line of fire that jumped from Lark's palm. It made it about halfway up the rock wall before dissipating.

"What—" Lark got no further before being interrupted by the guards overhead shooting into the surrounding forest.

"How many?" Harold dropped his lunch, grabbed Lark, and started pulling her toward the hoverbikes.

Conan scooped up Snowy and followed.

"At least fifty, and more are coming." The sentry called down.

"Go!" Harold's order boomed across the clearing.

"What's happening?" Lark asked in a shaky voice.

"We're under attack. Do you remember the plan?" Harold practically threw Lark onto her bike.

Lark nodded. They could now hear bodies crashing toward them through the trees.

Conan stuffed a protesting Snowy into Lark's backpack and then shoved it in her arms. He jumped onto his bike, the other decoy riders appearing beside him.

Harold slipped something into Lark's hand. Lark opened her fingers to reveal the wisteria tree on his bracelet softly pulsing with a light purple in her palm.

"Keep going down the mountain. The others will find you with this. I've also sent an emergency signal to the Capital. They'll send a team for you. Get home safely, my princess." Harold started to turn away.

"Wait!" Lark obviously didn't want to abandon them.

"Go!" Harold ordered, pulling his gun and firing white-hot lasers at the figures beginning to pour out of the trees.

"Let's go!" Conan called.

The four of them gathered at the top of the steep hill.

Taking one last look at his father, Conan spurred all of them forward. They peeled off in different directions once they were sure Lark was able to keep her seat.

Goodbye, dad.

CHAPTER 11

The three Spur Corps members moved down the hill with blinding speed. Even on a balanced hoverbike, Lark was nervous trying to keep up with them.

Don't break the handlebars! She forced her clenched fingers to loosen up.

Eyes tearing from the wind, Lark kept a sharp eye on Snowy in the backpack between her arms as her little group zigzagged through the trees. Passing branches slapped against her arms and legs.

It could've been her hearing playing tricks on her, but she began to suspect she was picking something up behind her. Something rising above the whistle of the gusts that were racing past her ears.

Please don't see anything. Please don't let there be anything behind me but trees.

Lark reluctantly turned her head.

Great. Just my luck.

Three someones were gaining on them via hoverbike. Lark's heartbeat thudded in her ears.

Conan also caught sight of their pursuers. With a subtle flick of his wrist, Lark's companions began to break off, one by one. She also changed directions so that it wasn't obvious they were trying to lead them away from her.

At first, it seemed to work. It looked like the pursuers had followed the Spur Corps members, not Lark. But pretty soon, the whizz of a red laser beam flew past her head, burning a smoking hole into a tree trunk ahead of them.

Startled, Lark jerked back and to the right. Her heart sank as she began to lose her balance.

"Ahh!" The wind swallowed Lark's scream as she tried to stay on the bike.

Another laser beam found its mark on Lark's right shoulder blade.

"Really?" Lark shouted, completely falling off now, but managing to keep her backpack and Snowy on the seat.

She felt embarrassed and angry at being shot by a laser and falling off a racing bike. Her heart beat wildly as she hit the ground with a thud, rolling until she crashed into a small river. It wasn't very deep, but it was cold. And irritating.

"Ouch!" Lark groaned. She scrambled out of the water, glaring at her pursuer. She couldn't tell if they were male or female. They had a bulky jacket on, and a tinted helmet concealed their face. They still had their gun pointed at her as they roared closer.

Thankfully, they ignored Lark's hovering bike, keeping their attention on her and not Snowy. It was just one; at least part of their plan to split up worked.

When her pursuer fired another laser beam at her, Lark jumped diagonally into a forward roll, thankful there was a decent amount of space between the trees here. Seemingly frustrated, the shooter circled Lark, pulling the trigger over and over, keeping her jumping around the forest floor.

"Would you stop shooting at me?" Lark finally roared. She suddenly remembered the lasers weren't going to hurt her. Deciding to simply let the lasers hit her, she stopped avoiding the beams. Lark's attacker came to a hovering standstill a few yards in front of her.

"You're the one!" A female voice sounded gleeful.

As her pursuer turned the hoverbike back uphill, Lark realized she knew she had the bio-bots and was probably going to tell whoever was in charge. Knowing she couldn't let her assailant leave, Lark sprang forward, tackling her off the bike and to the ground.

The women rolled away from each other, each taking a defensive stance. Lark automatically lowered her chin to give her neck extra protection. Forgetting her new physical abilities, Lark relied on her years of training. With frightening speed, Lark slammed her boot into her opponent's head, shattering the helmet and snapping her neck unnaturally. The limp body crashed into a tree several yards away before falling to the ground, motionless.

Aside from a slight sting in her foot—which only lasted a moment—Lark was unharmed but surprised at the damage she had wrought. Running over to the body, Lark checked for a pulse on the wrist, since the neck was shredded from the broken pieces of helmet. Nothing.

Lark's breath hitched. Yes, this person had been trying to kill her. Lark had acted in self-defense. But...she was dead! Lark had been in lots of little fights and scraps. In the moment of action, she could be cold, ruthless, and decisive. But after the dust settled...there it was. The shaking. The burning of holding tears at bay.

"I'm sorry," she whispered.

Flashes of memories assaulted her. Pain in her head. Cold, hard tile floor that was stained red with blood. Large hands heavy on her throat. Squeezing the life out of her.

Before she could hyperventilate for too long, Snowy's sharp cry pierced through the haze. She was still on Lark's hoverbike up the hill, trying to claw her way out of Lark's backpack.

Lark drew a deep, shuddering breath, then came back to calm Snowy down before she brought the whole horde of attackers on them. Snowy clambered onto Lark's shoulders, refusing to budge. At least she had quieted down.

After climbing back on the hoverbike, Lark mulled over their options.

She was sorely tempted to charge right back up the hill. She didn't know if there were more than fifty opponents her new friends were up against, but she knew even that was too many for any hope of victory. She didn't want anyone to sacrifice themselves for her. She felt guilty enough about Conan's burns.

Unfortunately, Harold had a point about her being a danger. Right now, she could just as easily hurt the very people she would try to protect. The weird incident with the fire leaping up from her palm at the beginning of the attack was proof of that.

Lark wasn't sure how yet, but she had made the flames jump. Once she knew how to utilize her new abilities, she would be a force to be reckoned with. But until then—

She paused, realizing something. *It seems I've accepted this as my new home, even if it's mostly out of necessity.*

Lark squeezed Harold's bracelet tighter. First, she needed to rejoin the other team. She could take her next steps from there.

"All right, girly." Lark nuzzled Snowy's head. "We've got to keep moving."

Steele frowned at the scene in front of him. Despite strict orders that he wanted everyone alive, he was currently looking at two dead bodies from the Wysteria Corps. Or were they Wysteria? Their identifying bracelets had an added flower on the engraving. A new military unit they weren't aware of yet?

Steele shook his head, a lock of light brown hair falling over his eye. Hmm. He would need to get a cut when he got back. Staying clean-shaven out here was simple, but there wasn't much he could do about his hair.

Turning toward the waiting soldiers behind him, he pretended not to notice their flinching. They should be scared. He was furious not only about having two dead bodies to deal with, but two of their quarries had also slipped through their fingers.

"Cover them in preservation wrap and leave them with the prisoners."

"Yes sir!" Everyone scattered to escape his intense gaze.

His lucky streak had obviously run out, since none of their hostages were The Weapon, as Casimer liked to call them. No one showed advanced healing when he did a small experimental cut on their forearm. He had been told The Weapon had superior strength and healing abilities. Since strength is easily disguised, this was the only way he could think of to quickly rule out candidates.

Steele made his way toward the hostages trapped inside a clear force field. After a short study, he came to a decision and turned to his current lieutenant.

"Keep them awake throughout the night. No food, only a little water. We start interrogations tomorrow."

Shamira gunned her hoverbike, following the blinking red dot on her map. Princess Larkspur should be just through those trees—aha!

"Your highness!" Shamira waved, although Lark had already spotted her.

"Shamira." Lark gave her a tight smile as she pulled up alongside her, Snowy looking remarkably relaxed wrapped around Lark's neck, paws dangling over her shoulders.

"We came to find you as soon as we saw the commander's beacon." Shamira gave Lark a once-over, making sure she was okay.

"I left them behind, Shamira." Lark sounded so guilty.

Shamira shook her head. "You did the right thing. A hoverplane is waiting for you about five minute's ride away."

"Did anyone else make it back?" Lark followed Shamira out of the woods.

Shamira paused before answering. "Only Raphael." Only two out of their ten-man-team made it to safety.

Lark bit her lip. "Can you tell if anyone is still alive? I assume you can track them with their bracelets."

Shamira hesitated again. "We can't be certain about everyone, but most of them still have a heartbeat."

"How many might be...might not...?" Lark's voice sounded dull and empty.

Shamira glanced back at Larkspur's stony face. "Possibly two or three. I'm sorry. We can't track the commander general's vitals without his bracelet, but Commander Conan is still alive."

Lark remained silent until they got back to the waiting caravan.

After Shamira introduced her to General Samuel and the two Spur Corps units that came with the hoverplane to pick her up, Lark dropped a bomb. "I'm not leaving yet."

"Your highness." General Samuel frowned. "We have orders—"

"And I'm changing them. We're rescuing my people. Only Commander General Cynbel is without his bracelet. Surely we can get a location from one of the other seven."

"Princess Larkspur." Raphael came to stand beside Shamira. "Of course a rescue will be mounted for two of our highest military commanders. But our first priority is your safety."

"Oh, no." Lark's eyes flashed with determination. "I just spent the last few hours running away, leaving behind men who put their lives on the line for me. You want me to accept the mantle of being your future ruler? Fine. But how can I call myself a leader if I leave my own people behind when I had a chance of saving them? With two extra units, that brings our numbers to over seventy. Certainly enough to mount that rescue."

General Samuel, Raphael, and Shamira all opened their mouths to protest, but Larkglared at them. They all retreated a tiny bit as Lark's back straightened with conviction. Shamira's eyes widened as she caught sight of Lark's hands. Was that blue lightning stirring around her fingers?

"None of you are strong enough to stop me. If your priority is to keep me safe, then help me bring our team home."

Everyone looked at each other. Shamira wondered if anyone else was feeling as inspired as she was. Lark was going to make a great queen.

"We are going to need reconnaissance," General Samuel finally said. "We know where they are, but we don't know what we're up against.

"There were at least fifty charging us," Raphael volunteered. "I didn't see much before we had to split, but they didn't seem like a uniform army. More like a band of well-armed mercenaries."

"General Samuel." Lark turned to him. "As you and Shamira are the highest-ranking officers here, work together to figure out what we need and how to get it."

"What will you be doing?" Shamira asked.

Lark studied her hands that were still covered with blue lightning. "I'm going to experiment as much as I can. I semi-controlled the flames last time. Let's see what else I can do."

CHAPTER 12

Harold sat silently, taking in everything around him, despite not getting a wink of sleep all night. After being roughly escorted to a large network of caves in the mountain, the prisoners were contained in a shimmery force field in one of the larger caverns. There, they were allowed to address their wounds as best they could. Aside from the two dead corps members, a couple broken bones and dislocated joints seemed to be the worst of the injuries.

Harold had been distracted from his hunger last night when Conan's bracelet started pulsing with a coded message saying their rescue was being mounted today. The signal was weak, so there was probably some sort of shielding up, but no one had better technology than Franklin's department made. Harold and his group gave the layout of how to get to them from the cave entrance, and everyone sent more information as they discovered things. The one good thing about them being kept up all night, Harold was finally getting a clue as to who they were dealing with.

They saw lots of people passing by, all armed to the teeth with laser guns and every type of blade imaginable. They seemed like mercenaries rather than a military unit. But they all answered to someone named Commander Steele Jones.

First, there were mumblings about Crofton, so Harold wondered if they were connected to Franklin's attack; if so, how did they get to them so quickly? But then he heard the name Talbot, and his heart sank. He still wasn't sure how they had been found, but it sounded like Casimer was finally making his move.

Harold tried to clamp down on the anger rising in him. He had told Avi there needed to be stricter surveillance on Casimer. Avi was a wise king, except in one area. When it came to his family, he was idiotically soft.

He understood why Avi didn't want to lose his only living relative, but Casimer had held his own uncle hostage, for crying out loud. And all Avi did was severely cut back his allowance and banish Casimer to his southern territory. Which wasn't exactly a hardship, as it was a naturally rich, sprawling hundred acres. So what if he wasn't allowed to leave for the rest of his life? He should be rotting in prison right now, at the very least.

Harold tried to loosen his clenched jaw as he saw someone approaching their group huddled against the cold stone wall. With at least four guns pointed at them, a small opening appeared in the force shield.

"You." One of them pointed at Harold. "The commander wants to see you."

His men watched as Harold's hands were tied behind his back and he slowly followed his guide under gunpoint. As they went deeper into the network of caves and tunnels, Harold tried to memorize the route, making note of any detail he could relay to the rescue team.

Stealing glances into passageways and caverns they passed, he didn't see much in the way of supplies or gear. Either their group traveled light, or they were stored somewhere else. Every few feet there were hovering orbs of light that gave a harsh glow to the dark stone. Eventually, his guard stopped in front of a dark brown, scratchy-looking blanket drawn across an opening to their left.

"Commander? I've brought the commander general."

"Let him in," said a deep voice.

The blanket was held aside, and Harold entered a small cave. The blanket dropped behind him, and he faced a fit young man standing behind a small table. Commander Jones looked to be in his late twenties, with a lean, muscular build and skin tanned from many hours in the sun. Some of his dark hair was falling into his gray eyes. Before it turned into a staring contest, Steele gestured toward an empty chair in front of his little table.

"Please sit." Steele was awfully polite for being the one in charge of attacking them.

Harold swept his gaze around the small alcove, taking as much in as he could without looking suspicious. A neatly made cot sat against the wall, a large backpack lay at the foot. On the table, there were stacked papers turned over so it was impossible to see what was on them. A rectangular, black VPhone sat next to a plate of half-eaten, juicy fruit. A silver bottle probably held some sort of drink.

Steele was obviously at home in these Spartan conditions. The only thing that separated him from his men was his commanding air and the fact that he had a bit more room to himself. This was a man who knew how to move swiftly and could work on minimalistic rations.

"Commander General Harold Cynbel." Steele sounded it out once they were sitting across from each other.

Harold stayed silent.

"What are you doing way out here, with such a small group? Did I interrupt an exercise by any chance?" Steele actually looked a little worried, but his voice remained calm and casual.

"What do you want?" Harold was too tired to play mind games.

"What do you think I want?" Steele tilted his head, eyes widening slightly in innocence.

Harold swallowed a laugh. He actually kind of liked this kid. Fine. He wanted to play? How about hardball. Might as well try to get some information himself.

Steele might be willing to talk if he thinks I'll reveal more than him. Unless being relatively easy on us as prisoners is all a game, he might be a decent guy.

"Who do you work for?" Harold asked.

"Who do you think I work for?" Steele replied.

"Casimer Talbot," Harold said promptly.

Steele winced, to Harold's surprise, then gave a tight smile.

"Very good, commander general." Steele looked admiring. "You are every bit as impressive as your reputation says. I do take orders from Talbot," he said with a glower.

Harold's eyebrows went up in surprise. Did Steele just spit out Casimer's name?

"For being so high up in the command, you don't seem to like your boss very well," Harold said, not sure if this was an act for his benefit.

Steele snorted derisively.

Still unsure, Harold said thoughtfully, "While I can see Casimer wanting someone of your skill, you don't really strike me as someone similar to him."

The gray eyes grew stormy. "Do not compare me to Talbot!" Steele thundered. "I am nothing like him. I see through his pompous ego."

Either he was the best actor Harold had ever seen, or Steele absolutely loathed Casimer's guts. Maybe even more than Harold.

"Then why are you his commander?" Harold asked. "Why would you stay if you hate him so much?"

There was a long, tense moment before Steele said in a tight voice, "I don't have a choice."

Glancing quickly at the blanket blocking the passageway, Harold leaned forward. "Maybe I can help."

"You can help," Steele said in a stony voice, "by telling me where to find the—the one with the bio-bots."

There was a slight pause before he said bio-bots, making Harold wonder if he had to think about what they were called. Harold really wanted to find out more about Steele and his situation, but one look at his face, and Harold knew now was not the time.

"All I know," Harold shook his head, "is they're far away from here."

"I'm sure, at the very least, you could find out where they are," Steele said, then held up a hand before Harold could say anything. "I know, I know. You wouldn't dream of it. Well—"

Steele was interrupted by his VPhone vibrating. Glancing down, he tapped it lightly, and a white bar appeared above it.

That's all Harold could see, but he knew Steele was reading a message on the other side.

With a look of irritation, Steele called for someone to take Harold away.

"I would very much appreciate you thinking about how to help me find The Weapon," Steele said as Harold was escorted out of his alcove. "I would hate for you to lose any more men."

Lark stared in awe at the hoverplane's control room as she and Snowy stayed tucked away in the corner, trying to stay out of the way. And not accidentally fry anything.

At first sight of the huge hovercraft—that she had taken to calling "The Mothership" in her head—Lark's jaw nearly dropped. It was about the size of a small cruise ship. How on earth did this thing get in the air?

When Shamira motioned for her to come, Lark followed her down a maze of hallways to a small, sparsely furnished bedroom.

"Snowy can stay here during the extraction," Shamira said.

"Thank you." Lark kissed Snowy's silky head, then put her down on the bed. Snowy hopped down and happily followed the girls to the door. "Ah, no Snowy." Lark felt horribly guilty leaving the cub by herself, but there was no way the cub could come on the mission.

Snowy's look of confusion when Lark closed the door in the cub's face nearly had Lark changing her mind. Then the howling started. Shamira and Lark shared a grimace, then ran away like the weaklings they apparently were.

"Are you ready?" Shamira asked as they grabbed their equipment and headed to the hangar that housed a fleet of smaller hovercrafts.

Lark ignored the ache in her chest. She imagined she could still hear Snowy's plaintive cries even though they were on the other side of the hoverplane. "I'm as ready as I can be," she finally said.

"You just concentrate on your part," Shamira said confidently. "Leave the rest to us."

CHAPTER 13

"We have to get going." The holographic image of Steele's torso and head flicked for a moment. "I haven't finished the interrogations, but we've picked up a hoverplane on our radar."

"Didn't you search for trackers?" Casimer berated Steele.

Steele's eyes flashed with annoyance. "Yes, I did. And our shields are up. But there's always a possibility that Doctor Wright has invented a stronger signal into something we don't know about."

"Did you at least get any useful information?"

"Not yet."

Before Casimer could respond with anything more than a scowl, Steele turned his head toward some disturbance behind him.

"Sir, we need you!" a voice called from someone Casimer couldn't see.

"I have to go." Steele looked so stern, Casimer didn't even protest as the vid-call link was cut and Steele's image dissolved into thin air.

Casimer breathed deeply, trying to quell his boiling rage. Turning to his office's only other occupant, he couldn't help pounding his desk while growling, "Nothing's going right, Beck!"

"Steele has done well, all things considered, sir," Beck said. "We wouldn't have anything right now if it weren't for his quick actions."

Casimer reluctantly acknowledged the truth of Beck's words.

"But this does leave us in a precarious position," Beck continued. "It seems Vusal already knows about Crofton's involvement in the attack on Doctor Wright. They're not doing anything yet, but we don't know how long that will last. We have to assume Crofton's support of you, and the extent of your coup, will be revealed sooner than planned."

Franklin Wright was supposed to be the price for the backing of an experienced army from That Woman. Without that guarantee, Crofton was their strongest ally. Crofton's Prime Minister was an old school chum of Casimer's and was the first to pledge help for his cause. After promises of vast territories and resources, of course.

"You should think about moving the timeline up," Beck advised.

Casimer gave a sharp nod. "Speed up the preparations. I have to call...her." Casimer grimaced. "I don't know yet what she will want now that Franklin is gone. But we need her army. Let me know when my territory is ready to defect to Crofton. Call Steele. Tell him to get everyone here as quickly as possible. Also, keep Commander General

Cynbel and his son. It's unlikely they'll break easily, but at the very least they will be valuable hostages. Get rid of the rest."

ϞϞϞ

Harold glanced at his men. They were ready. Their rescue attempt should be happening any moment now.

There was a buzz from the guards around them and throughout the cave. Cries of "hovercraft!" "move!" and "watch out!" echoed along the stone walls.

Harold tensed, not sure what to expect next.

Steele came running around a corner just as the shimmery force field around them turned blurry and started to shift. Steele's look of confusion was the last thing Harold saw before the electric wall moved to create a crooked path for the prisoners, as well as trap Steele and his men inside the cave.

"What is going on?" Steele's angry voice rang out from behind the blurry wall of white-hot electricity.

Someone was either foolish enough to try and touch it, or they got pushed into its path. Either way, their screams told everyone to steer clear of the blurry, wavy walls, now acting as their shield.

"Let's move!" Harold helped to carry one of their dead comrade's bodies.

Their group didn't hobble far before several of the rescue team found them.

"We've got you, commander general." Samuel came up to help support Harold.

Before Harold could say or ask anything, the blurry force field started to pulse and waver.

"That can't be good," Conan said through a split lip.

"Move as fast as you can!" Harold barked. "Get out of this cave!"

Passing by the still bodies of their enemies lying scattered across the ground, they made their way to the cave entrance, their force field shield going more haywire with every step. By the time they were in fresh air and sunshine, there were sparks flying everywhere.

"That's the last of us!" Samuel shouted to someone above the cave entrance.

"Thank goodness." Lark sounded exhausted. She was holding onto something on top of the rocks. "Hurry and get everyone on the hovercraft. I can't keep this up much longer!" She grunted.

"What is going on? Why is she here?" Harold hissed.

"No time, sir." Samuel dragged him toward the hovercraft.

⚡⚡⚡

Sweat poured down Lark's temples. She stood on top of the large cave entrance where their attackers had set up a row of small black solar panels to soak up the sunshine. Controlling all this electric energy from one of the solar power conductors was taking way more out of her than she had hoped. It should have been scorching to the touch, but Lark just felt a calming warmth.

The roof she, Shamira, and another Spur Corps member stood on was about three meters above the ground and roughly ten meters wide, with rock walls reaching for the sky at their backs and to their left.

Lark's bodyguards dumped the bodies of some attackers over the side. Lark was thankful they were covering her back so she could focus on her task. She wanted to give the rest of them cover as long as possible so they could safely board their escape vehicles. Her own was waiting above their heads, ropes dangling at the ready for a speedy ascent.

Terrible pain ate at Larkspur from the inside out. She was getting lightheaded. Her skin felt like it was crawling and tightening at the same time. Very unnerving.

Just a little longer.

She watched the last of their team disappearing into the surrounding forest. There were several small hovercrafts rising above the trees all around them. Lark glanced to her side, having the itchy feeling she was being watched. But the enhanced vision she was starting to get used to was gone. As the energy in her hand started to waver, she turned back to the conductor in front of her.

"Everything is becoming too unstable." She coughed up blood, watching it bloom on the ground in front of her with a detached feeling.

"Lark!" Shamira jumped forward, worry lacing her voice.

Lark barely registered spitting out more blood before she lost all control and a tremendous explosion beneath their feet knocked her into blackness.

✦✦✦

When the main cave opening was blocked off with a blurry force field, Steele ordered everyone to grab what they could and evacuate, then ran to the alcove he had been using as an office and bedroom.

What sort of weapon can manipulate force fields to this degree?

He had never heard of anything like this. Rummaging through a bag, he pulled out a pale cloak, threw it around his shoulders, grabbed his emergency pack, and made his way to a small back exit. Anything with an active electrical current was going haywire. Sparks flew from the lighting orbs lining the cave walls. He threw his VPhone away when it began throwing off sparks.

When he emerged from the back of the cave, he saw a small hovercraft waiting near the cave entrance about a hundred yards away. He left his pack under a bush and activated the camouflage function of his cloak as he started toward the front of the cave.

Going slowly to make sure his cloak was still working properly, Steele got about twenty yards away from the cave entrance when his group of hostages came stumbling out into the fresh air. He froze.

"That's the last of us!" One of the men on the ground called up to the cave roof.

Steele looked up to see three figures grouped on top of the cave entrance. Two females and a male.

"Thank goodness!" The dark-haired woman nearly gasped from exhaustion. She was holding onto one of their power conductors. Was she the one causing this mess?

Steele quietly scaled the rocky side of the cave, poking his camouflaged head over the side to get a better look at the trio.

What in the world?

What was that around the dark-haired woman's hands? Blue electricity writhed around her arms. Her exposed skin looked to be rippling as it faded from opaque black to pale skin with veins bulging, and back to a shimmery, scaly opaque black again.

As if she sensed him staring at her, the woman glanced his way just as he reached for his laser gun. Not daring to breathe, he froze, unable to tear his gaze away from her face. A sapphire blue right eye and metallic silver left eye seemed lit from within, creating a mesmerizing, unearthly glow.

His head pounded and his heart raced. Why? He didn't know her, did he?

Voices muffled in hazy memories. Feelings of purpose, of love. Blinding pain nearly caused Steele to let go of his perch and fall three meters to the hard ground. Grunting softly, he clambered up onto the cave roof, still a good ten yards away from the others.

"Lark!"

The name pulled at something inside him. Steele looked up just in time to see the red-haired woman and her male companion jump forward to grab hold of the dark-haired enigma.

Feeling an intense need to help her, Steele almost threw off his camouflage cloak when a huge wave of that blue electricity flew from the woman's hands and licked its way into the ground. A large explosion from the cave rocked everyone.

Steele was knocked backward, and a new spasm of agony kept him sprawled on his rocky hideout. He could only watch as the man and red-haired woman gathered themselves together, carrying Steele's unconscious dark-haired woman to the waiting harnesses that lifted them into the hovercraft.

"Wait," he gasped, hand stretching out toward the disappearing vehicle.

He lay still, panting, letting his wits come back to him, until he realized the vibrations and rumblings beneath him were cave-ins. He scrambled to get his sore body clear of the cave, pulled himself together, and rounded up the stragglers of his group to send them in search of other survivors. If they couldn't manage to get back into the cave, they would have a lot of equipment and supplies to replace.

He spent the next few hours rescuing people and retrieving bodies from the ruined network of cave tunnels, organizing lists, and deciding what he was—and wasn't— going to tell Casimer.

CHAPTER 14

Harold joined Conan, Shamira and Raphael at Lark's side in the hoverplane's medical section. Harold wasn't sure why he bothered glancing at the scan readouts Raphael was pouring over. It was all just a jumble of medical terms and numbers to him.

He apparently got too close to Lark's unconscious form for Snowy's liking. The tiny tiger puffed up, hissed, and made a vicious swipe for Harold's arm. Seeming to understand Lark's current vulnerability, Snowy had stationed herself on Lark's bed as her feisty guardian, only allowing Shamira, Conan, and Raphael near her without bared fangs.

Not wanting his arm shredded by Snowy's claws, Harold took a step back toward Raphael, Snowy's predatory stare following his every move.

"How is she? What happened?" Harold asked Raphael.

"I don't know what happened to her," Raphael said grimly. "I can only make guesses based off of what I've seen since we got here."

"And that is?" Conan squinted at Lark's unconscious form through a black eye.

Instead of answering Conan, Raphael turned to Shamira. "What exactly did she do?"

"She used one of their power conductors to manipulate their force field. Since you had given us rough distances to the exit, that's what she went off of. But she had only just started to figure out how to move energy, so there's no telling what else she affected."

"We don't know her limits yet," Raphael said gravely. "What worries me is her organs looked like they were eating themselves up either before the bio-bots kicked in, or they were deteriorating too fast for the bio-bots to keep up. But now her body is repairing itself at a remarkable rate. These bio-bots are really something else."

"Will she be all right?" Harold asked.

"I can't guarantee anything since we just don't know how badly she pushed herself or how thorough the bio-bots are. But, if things keep going the way they are now, she should physically be perfectly fine very soon."

Everyone gave a sigh of relief.

"How are you all doing?" Shamira asked her commanding officers.

"We'll be fine," Harold assured her. "Let's get our princess home."

Pain. Head splitting. Pressure closing around the throat.

Can't breathe!

Tears streaming down cheeks, noiseless sobs wracking a tiny frame.

Blood everywhere.

Help. Someone. Anyone.

Help!

Lark jerked awake and flew into a sitting position. She just barely swallowed a scream. One of her own hands was wrapped around her throat, the other stretched in front of her. She wasn't sure if she was trying to fend something off or reach out for help. Heart racing, blood pounding in her ears, she gasped for breath.

"Lark? I mean, princess."

The deep voice caused her to jump and whirl around to face whoever else was with her. Her movements ended up twisting sheets and blankets around her body.

She had just enough time to register Conan as the room's other occupant before a yowl of protest scared her enough to let out a short, breathless scream. Poor Snowy had apparently been resting either beside or on top of Lark and was now just as tangled in the sheets.

"Lark, are you okay? What's wrong?" Conan jumped up from a plump chair in the corner.

"No!" Not completely back in the present, she shrank away, hands flying to her throat.

She closed her eyes and breathed deep, attempting to pull her wits together. She hadn't had this nightmare for a couple months. She wasn't going to count her mini panic attack after the scuffle in the woods. Shuddering, she managed to force her hands down. She couldn't afford to show anyone her greatest fear. Maybe she could smooth this over somehow.

"I'll be fine." Lark absolutely hated how breathless her voice sounded. "I had a nightmare. It's nothing."

Conan wasn't an idiot. But he didn't comment.

"Are *you* okay?" She looked him over.

His left eye was nearly swollen shut and a ghastly shade of dark purple, ringed by a small circle of green. It looked like his lip had been split, and his right arm was in a sling. A head bandage covered some of his blond locks.

"Nothing permanent." He smiled. "My shoulder was dislocated briefly, but this is just so I don't overuse it while it's recuperating."

Lark carefully untangled herself and Snowy from the blankets.

"Shamira told us what you said." Conan sounded a little awkward. "Thank you for coming back for us." His sky-blue eyes held her gaze for a moment before he bowed. "I'll get the doctor."

Lark watched him leave silently. She got the feeling he was giving her a private moment to calm down.

Conan was smart, so he'd eventually catch on that she protected her neck vigorously when they started sparring. She could work her way out of almost any situation. But when something tightened around her throat, she froze. She couldn't move, couldn't think, couldn't do anything. Sometimes she catatonic for hours, barely able to move or comprehend anything. Other times, her panic grew until she just screamed and then curled up in a sobbing ball.

No matter how much she trained, it never got better. Learning the basics of jiujitsu was torture. She greatly preferred practicing Thai boxing and kicking. She had strong legs.

Wondering where she was, Lark glanced around the room. It looked like the most luxurious hospital ward she had ever seen. The bare, whitewashed walls gave it a sterile feeling, but her large bed had silk sheets. There was a deep sink, counter, and light maple cabinets catty-corner from her bed. Some sort of action movie was being projected high on the white wall across from her, but she couldn't see a remote to turn the sound on.

There were small, sticky dots on her chest, abdomen, and head. No wires, but she could feel a faint electrical pulse from them.

Snowy plopped into her lap and waved her tiny paws up at her.

Lark massaged her throat one more time, then allowed the last vestiges of fear to be replaced by amusement. Thanks to playing with Snowy, she was able to face the group that came in with smiles and laughter. Conan opened the door, followed by Raphael, Harold, Shamira, an unknown man that looked close to her age, and King Avi.

He looked almost exactly like he did in her memories. Thick, snow-white hair, long nose, copper-colored eyes. His tall frame might be slightly pudgier than she remembered.

Somehow, his enthusiastic air made her angry.

կկկ

Avi's heart warmed as he noticed how much Larkspur had matured in the last few years, and a mix of emotions flooded him as he caught sight of her. Relief that she was awake, excitement that she was finally here, worry about how she would settle in. Then an icy coldness clenched his heart when her beaming smile vanished upon seeing him, and her eyes flashed with anger.

"H-hello, Larkspur." Avi wasn't even sure what his voice sounded like.

"Sir." Lark's tight nod and cold voice felt like a hammer.

I messed up. Again.

He had so hoped to do things right with Larkspur. But obviously, he had made a huge mistake along the way.

As soon as Raphael proclaimed Lark completely recovered, Avi ordered everyone out. They needed to talk. But when they were alone, an oppressive silence hung between then.

"Harold told me about Snowy," Avi finally spoke up.

Lark glanced tenderly at the tiger cub curled up sleeping on her lap. "I'm told I can keep her because you adopted me."

"We searched and searched, but you simply disappeared," Avi blurted. He hated how it sounded like he was scrambling for an excuse. He took a deep breath and continued with a calmer cadance. "I was trying to meet you and your brothers to talk about my wish to adopt all of you. But time travel is still a spotty business, even more so back then. I had to return to this time before I could find you, and we were unsuccessful in later attempts to hit the right time and place."

"Why me?" Lark asked bluntly.

"Which part? The bio-bots or the adoption?" Avi gave a small smile.

"All of it, I guess." Lark shrugged. "Why did you even want to adopt us? You knew us for two weeks."

Avi hesitated. Would she hate him even more if he told the whole truth now? Well, he would tell her most of it, anyway.

"I've always wanted a family, but my queen and I were never blessed with children. One by one, I lost all my extended family members until my nephew, Casimer, was the sole survivor. He lost his parents at a young age. In my enthusiasm to be a loving parent figure, I forgot to be a good one. I was warned, but I refused to believe I had indulged him beyond the point of a spoiled brat. By the time I could no longer turn a blind eye, he was a man. I had wasted my one opportunity to be a father." Avi felt a wave of shame as he remembered his foolishness. "And then I met you. You and your brothers were exactly what I always dreamed of for my children. I thought I had found a second chance to do things right. I thought I could make up my mistakes with Casimer."

"You wanted to atone for the horrible person your nephew turned out to be, through us?" Lark's voice trembled with barely controlled anger.

"I'm sorry." As a powerful king respected throughout the galaxies, Avi was not used to admitting he could have been wrong.

"Where, exactly, did the bio-bots fit in this plan?" Lark didn't quite hide the sarcastic undertone.

Avi hesitated for a fraction too long. He couldn't tell her the real reason. Not yet. He couldn't admi—even to himself—how selfish his motives were. "I did, and still do, think you will make an excellent ruler. The bio-bots had to be entrusted to someone that wouldn't easily abuse their power. But they were also to help protect you."

Lark raised a dark eyebrow.

"The bio-bots weren't meant as a weapon, per se. The idea was for them to work as a shield, protecting the lives of our soldiers like never before. The unit who were to have them would be our Shield Unit. And who better to lead the country's shield than the reigning monarch?"

Lark didn't object, so Avi kept going.

"When we met, adversaries were closing in on all sides. It was imperative we keep the bio-bots out of enemy hands, so we programmed the bio-bots to your DNA using a sample of your blood. Once they're programmed, it's impossible to change, making them useless to anyone else."

"So, in the end, I was used as a convenience." Lark's low voice pierced Avi.

When he finally plucked up the courage to look at her, Avi was taken aback by her eyes. The darkened jewel tones were glowing.

For so long, he had studied those prophecies. He wanted his family to be the ones with "strength beyond compare." Even if it was through adoption, his family name would still go down in history. Now he realized there was a lot of work ahead of him if he wanted a relationship with Larkspur. Papers didn't make a family.

He just prayed Lark would be willing to let him try.

ϟϟϟ

"Thank you for your explanation. Is that all?" It took everything in Lark to not yell at Avi.

What kind of selfish, shortsighted, pompous jerk thought she would be okay with them experimenting with her DNA, dragging her into his problems, and using her precious family to atone for his own stupid mistakes?

But Avi was still a king. Her king, now, since she had agreed to stay. Even coming from a modern-day (or was it ancient now?) democracy, she knew you didn't just talk smack to a monarch, no matter how benevolent they might be.

126

"That's all for now." Avi's voice was calm and strong, despite the sorrow in his eyes. "I'm glad you are feeling better. Let me know if you need anything. I'll see you later, Larkspur."

She refused to be moved by his depressed departure. They would have to work out exactly what kind of relationship they were going to have later.

Snowy, sensing Lark's mood, jumped up and batted her face.

"Hang on, girl." Lark set the tiger on the bed beside her. "I've got a lot to think about. And I don't want to accidentally shock you."

Putting aside her ire for Stupid Avi for the moment, she had agreed to become his heir—even if that was mostly just to make it easier to rescue her brothers from their doomed past. And he apologized. Most likely, as a king, he didn't have to do that very often.

There was way too much she didn't know. Not just about herself, but about this new world she found herself in. There was no helping the past. She was here, she had the bio-bots. Unless something changed, she would shoulder the mantle of a kingdom in the future. And if she was honest, she was getting excited to explore. And there was no denying the bio-bots came with some advantages.

All right, first things first. Bio-bots, then time travel. She wanted to save her brothers, not accidentally electrocute them. The more she understood Franklin's invention, the better off she would be.

Right now, knowledge was power.

CHAPTER 15

Lark lifted her head at a soft knock on the door.

"Lark?" Conan popped his head in. "Is this a good time?"

It had been twenty minutes since Avi had left. Lark no longer felt like she was about to explode, so she smiled stiffly and nodded.

"Come on in." Lark stood up.

Conan was followed by Shamira and the stranger from before. Shamira ran to Lark and enveloped her in a hug, surprising both of them. She awkwardly took a step back from Lark.

"I'm so glad you're okay!" Shamira nearly cried. "You have no idea how scared I was when you *coughed up blood*!"

"I'm sorry." Lark scratched her neck. "I didn't mean to scare you. I'm not exactly sure what happened."

"I have an idea," the stranger piped up.

Shamira stepped aside so Lark could see him.

"This is the genius little brother I told you about, Joshua Cynbel." Conan draped his uninjured arm around Joshua's shoulders.

"I've been looking forward to meeting you!" Lark gave a genuine smile, shaking Joshua's hand enthusiastically. "I'm Larkspur Bei, but you can call me Lark."

"A pleasure to meet you, princess. And if I may point out, you are now Larkspur Kynaston." Joshua gave a slight bow. He wasn't cold, just...clinical. No smile, just a burning gaze that seemed to have as many questions as she did.

"Ah, right," Lark said. "I guess I am a Kynaston now, huh? Still not used to that name."

She studied Joshua, automatically comparing him with his brother. A little shorter than Conan's six-foot height and less muscular, though he was still fit. A resemblance in the strong jaw, angular nose, and high cheekbones were unmistakable. Joshua's dark blond hair was a shade darker than Conan's, almost a light brown. And Joshua had hazel eyes, as opposed to Conan's blue with green specks. They also lacked the warm, friendly look Conan now had for her.

Joshua wore slacks and a button-down shirt. Oddly formal next to everyone else, who wore casual pants, shorts, and loose shirts. He was also carrying the first real notebook and pen she had seen since coming to this time.

"Where are we?" Lark asked, distracting herself from comparing the Cynbel brothers.

"We're in Vusal, on the palace grounds," Shamira said.

"We're here?" Lark felt sorry she had missed seeing the city on their way in. "When can I go exploring?"

"You're still a secret," Joshua reminded her. "You can't leave the palace grounds yet. But that still gives you over a hundred acres to tour."

"One hundred acres?" Lark's jaw nearly dropped.

"The palace grounds were created to be completely self-sufficient," Conan said. "It's never happened, but the entire government could be under siege for years, and you'd be fine."

"Wow."

"You're in the hospital building, located behind the main palace," Shamira offered.

"This is a hospital room?" Lark looked around again. "It seemed like it, but it's way nicer than I've ever seen before."

"That reminds me, you said you had an idea of what happened to Lark?" Shamira asked Joshua.

Joshua tapped the notebook in his hand. "If I understand the scans correctly, you overextended yourself. The bio-bots can store a lot of energy, but it's not infinite. If you continue attempting to output energy after the stores are drained, they will turn to the next closest source. Your own body."

"I beg your pardon?" Lark looked down at herself, then back to Joshua, puzzled.

"Your body is made up of energy. It's practically a long-lasting battery. But it's also delicately balanced. If you continue to ask it for too much, it will shut down. Your organs were basically eating themselves up."

Shamira went even paler than she normally was. It made her fiery red hair and emerald eyes stand out even more.

"It's imperative we carefully learn your limits to ensure you don't endanger yourself again," Joshua lectured.

Lark nodded, feeling chastised.

"How are you feeling?" Joshua asked, looking between her and his open notebook.

Lark stretched, trying to internally gauge herself. "I feel perfect!"

Joshua nodded. "Excellent. Then we can start lessons tomorrow. I will be your tutor for the time being. I have enough of a grasp on most essentials to help you. For now, we'll do lessons in the morning, tests in the afternoon."

"Tests?" Lark raised her eyebrows.

"We need data on the bio-bots. We need to know your abilities and limits."

"Ah, those kinds of tests."

"With your permission, I'll take my leave." Joshua gave a small bow.

Lark blinked. "Um, sure. Thank you?"

She watched him exit the room, then turned to Conan. He was trying to stifle a laugh.

"Is he always like that?" Lark asked.

Knowing she was going to be spending nearly every waking minute with Joshua for the foreseeable future, and since he was family to Conan and Harold, Lark had hoped to be good friends with him, but the formality of his speech and bearing created a barrier. His detached gaze made her feel like science experiment or puzzle to him. Which, admittedly, she kind of was. But that didn't mean she enjoyed feeling like one.

"He warms up to people," Conan assured her.

"Sometimes," Shamira mumbled under her breath.

Lark shot her a look, then sighed. "Oh goody. This is going to be fun."

Lark's head was spinning, and she had only had two days of lessons. There was no end of facts, theories, names, numbers, and experimenting.

Finished with her break, Lark was walking Snowy on a leash and harness back to the classroom. Her earlier lessons swam around in her memory.

"We're still in the Milky Way, but a different solar system. It's named Verne, after Verne Sheridan, the man who discovered Evren was capable of being habitable." Lark had been mumbling all this under her breath, but as she opened the classroom door, she said triumphantly, "Evren is the third successfully terraformed planet!"

Thinking the classroom would be empty, Lark was surprised to find Joshua already there, typing something into his tablet.

The room was a converted office. An updated version of whiteboards hung along one wall—a projected screen hovered less than an inch from the wall, and instead of markers, you used a special stylus to write in the air. Two desks for Joshua and Larkspur sat next to the single window overlooking an orchard with a variety of trees. Maps, globes, notebooks, and papers were scattered around the room, with the occasional flickering hologram depending on the lesson.

In the corner, Snowy had a huge, fluffy bed and scratching post with food and water bowls ready for her use. There was even a litter box for when lessons went long and they didn't get a walk outside. So far, she hadn't disrupted class with curious explorations too much.

"Very good, your highness." Joshua stood up.

As he politely waited for her to take a seat, he launched straight into a twenty-minute lecture about astronomy, which Lark actually found interesting. She and her brothers would stargaze for hours back on Earth. But that reminded her.

"Um, Joshua?" Lark raised her hand. Why, she wasn't entirely sure. "Actually, you said we could talk about time travel after the break."

"Oh, that's right." Joshua nodded. "My apologies, your highness."

"Just Lark is fine. We're not doing any official functions right now," Lark said for what felt like the hundredth time.

"Thank you." Joshua bowed for what felt like the hundred and fiftieth time.

Giving up for today, Lark moved on. "So, there are time travel particles?"

"Yes. Doctor Franklin stumbled upon them as we were researching how to make teleportation easier and more energy efficient. He merely called them 'time travel particles,' but I am going to officially name them the 'Wright Particles.' I only wish I could make it public knowledge. His funeral is tomorrow, and no one will know about one of his greatest achievements."

The most dynamic part of Joshua, Lark had noted, were his hazel eyes. He hadn't cracked a smile for the last two days, but when he got excited about something, his eyes lightened almost to a honey gold. When he was lost in concentration or was mournful—like now—they grew dark.

"Well, from what I've seen, he is still highly respected as the brilliant man he was," Lark said, hoping to lighten Joshua's mood.

He only nodded his head silently.

"I'm sorry for your loss," Lark said gently. "I heard you two were really close."

Joshua's face softened, eyes getting a little wistful. "Grandpa Franklin and his experiments have been my life since I was twelve. I lost more than my mentor when he was killed."

Lark didn't know what to say, and Joshua seemed lost in memories. Lark sat quietly, wondering if she should try to comfort him somehow. But before she could awkwardly pat him on the shoulder, Joshua blinked, and he was back to his distant, clinical self.

"The Wright Particles travel around," Joshua said, moving on as if nothing had happened.

Lark was a little taken aback.

I thought we were getting somewhere. For a second there, I saw a human being. Not a science-crazy machine.

But he was getting back to time travel, which she needed to learn all she could about, so she pushed her frustration aside to focus. With Franklin gone, he was the only expert around.

"If they move, how do you find them?" Lark asked.

"I developed a scanner that targets the particles." Joshua sounded a little proud. "It lets us know how much is gathered where."

"Where does this information get sent?" Lark tried to sound casual.

Despite the fact that she asked endless questions about all her different lessons so far, Joshua glanced at her with narrowed eyes. "It comes to a program on my tablet," he finally said.

Lark endeavored not to look too greedily at the small rectangle device sitting on his desk. It had a touch screen, although he preferred a stylus, and holographic capabilities.

Asking if that was the only place to find the information would most likely be a dead giveaway for what she wanted to do. Well, so would her next question, probably. But it also seemed like a logical thing to ask.

"Are there limitations to when someone can travel to?"

Look innocent, look innocent! You're just a pure-hearted, curious student.

Joshua didn't answer for an agonizing minute. Just looked at her thoughtfully.

Please don't tell me I blew it.

Lark resisted fidgeting nervously. She highly doubted using the top secret time travel technology for a trip to save her brothers would be approved. So doing it first and asking forgiveness later was the path she had chosen.

Joshua finally continued in a lecturing tone. "We're not sure of a time or distance limit yet. But we do know you shouldn't go back on your own timeline."

Lark felt her heart crash and didn't think she could quite manage to keep it off her face. "Why is that? Does it change the future?"

"The man who tested it several times complained of a bad headache that worsened each trip."

"That's all? Just a headache?"

Hope made her heart start thumping in her chest. She was thankful Joshua didn't have enhanced hearing. If all it did was mess with her head a little, the bio-bots would probably take care of that. And even if they didn't, she would gladly live with head pain for the rest of her life if it meant Alex and Sterling were alive and well.

"It did something to his brain," Joshua said, giving Lark pause. "We don't know what exactly, or how bad it could become, because he ended up dying in an unfortunate accident. After that, King Avi forbade any time travel within one's own lifetime."

Sobered, Lark pondered thoughtfully, but not for too long. Really, to see her brothers again, she would take that risk.

Joshua pointed to the clock on the wall. "I have preparations to make for Director Wright's funeral tomorrow. Instead of tests this afternoon, Conan will take you on a tour of the palace, perhaps even some of the grounds if you have time. I'm sure you'd like to see more than this room, the dining room, and your suite of rooms."

Lark looked at Joshua, astonished. He still didn't crack a smile, but was that a joke he just said?

"He should be here any moment," Joshua said. "We'll pick up on time travel in a few days."

"Thanks." She smiled.

She heard footsteps coming down the hall and turned to hook Snowy back onto her leash. They opened the door to Conan, hand up ready to knock.

"Hey!" Conan grinned. "You guys ready for your tour?"

"Ready!" Lark said, walking down the hall.

She heard Conan remind Joshua about dinner and her step faltered. Conan and Harold had invited her to join them for dinner, and she had accepted earlier.

Duh. Of course it would make sense for Joshua to be there, too. Oh goody.

CHAPTER 16

Joshua listened to his brother and the princess walk away from the classroom, then turned to his desk, deep in thought. Princess Larkspur would need to become a better actress. She wouldn't make a very good queen if everything she thought appeared on her face. Then again, he was a sharper observer than most people. Still, it had been blatantly obvious why the princess was so interested in time travel. She practically bubbled over with enthusiasm. He had also noticed her determined gaze after he warned of the dangers.

He had debated telling Princess Larkspur how to find the Wright Particles. But he was curious about what she would do with the information he gave her.

Everyone knew about the dead princes. King Avi had been so excited when he announced the adoption of the three siblings. He was equally devastated when their research brought up their obituaries.

There was no doubt he cared about them. But Joshua had begun to suspect the king had a secret agenda for adopting the Bei siblings. He was awfully insistent on an heir he only really knew for a couple weeks.

He wasn't sure what to make of the crown princess yet.

I wonder how far she'll go for her brothers.

⚡⚡⚡

Lark followed Conan down the hallway. They all looked the same: soft white walls, purple trim, the occasional picture to break up the monotony. She wondered if it was for uniformity or to help unwanted intruders get lost.

The palace was huge, with a five-story main building and four-story east and west wings. They descended from the main building's fourth-floor offices to meet Shamira in the grand lobby. The shiny marble floor stretched from the ornate front door to a grand, sweeping staircase leading to a second-floor balcony. A huge chandelier cast a soft glow over the whole area.

"Thanks for showing me around!" Lark said as she and Conan joined Shamira at the foot of the stairs.

Conan's arm was still in a sling and his bruised eye was still discolored, but his head bandage was gone. Since they were all off duty, everyone wore casual clothes, which looked out of place in the opulent lobby.

"Of course," Conan said.

"No problem." Shamira grinned.

"I love your hair!" Lark almost reached out to touch Shamira's head without thinking.

"Thank you." Shamira tossed the end of her inside-out French braid over her shoulder. "I have younger sisters, and we play with each other's hair all the time."

"I've always been too lazy to do much more than throwing it in a bun or ponytail." Lark reached up to her bunned dark tresses self-consciously.

"I'd be happy to teach you," Shamira offered.

"I'd love that!"

They followed Conan through a door to the left of the lobby.

"This is the press room," Conan said.

The room had about fifty chairs, all pointed toward a small stage at the back of the room. That wall was covered with a huge, colored version of the Kynaston family crest.

"This is where you'll first be introduced to Lothar," Shamira announced, sending Lark's knees knocking.

She gulped, thinking about being the center of all that attention.

This is for Alex and Sterling. This is for Alex and Sterling.

Becoming crown princess of Lothar was in large part so she could have access to the knowledge and technology needed to save her brothers. Lark cringed inwardly. Even to her that sounded like a terribly selfish reason to lead a country. She vowed then and there to be the best leader she could be to make it up to her new home and friends.

It'll be worth it. Just keep your eyes on the prize.

She enjoyed the tour, although they couldn't even get through the whole palace, much less any of the grounds. After the press room, they entered the east wing. They ignored the top floors that were filled with empty guest rooms and instead explored the entertainment-dedicated ground floor. Lark oohed and aahed at the large, personal theater room large enough to seat one hundred and fifty people.

"Oh, this is going to be fun! I've got two thousand years of movies to catch up on!" Lark only half joked.

When she asked about the absence of staff, Conan explained most of the cleaning and mundane chores were done by robots. There were hired humans for the kitchen staff, stables, and driving. She was avoiding the kitchen until she was officially announced, and no one besides the Wysteria and Spur Corps were allowed in the west wing where the family rooms were located. She hadn't been anywhere else besides the fourth floor for class and tests until today.

The giant ballroom and dining hall took up the second floor of the main building. Dark wood floors and molding complemented the ornate, jewel-toned decorations. Small chandeliers added to the sparkling, festive feel of the rooms.

Shamira bid farewell when they descended to the first floor again, citing a previous dinner engagement.

Lark followed Conan to the private dining hall next to the first floor kitchen, where they found Harold and Joshua waiting for them over a steaming dinner of roasted quail, seasonal vegetables, and some sort of pink pasta dish with a creamy, sky-blue sauce.

Lark's mouth watered.

They dug in, casual conversation tossed around between bites. With Franklin's funeral the next day, the discussion naturally turned to him.

"I'm sorry I can't come to the service," Lark said. Sometimes, having a secret existence could be a real problem.

"I set up cameras today so you can watch on your tablet," Joshua said, nonchalantly spearing a piece of meat.

She looked up at him from her plate. That was part of his preparations? "Thank you," she said, her heart warming. She wasn't as close with Franklin as the Cynbels were, but she did remember him fondly. It meant a lot that she could still be part of his memorial service.

"And you can always visit his mausoleum after everyone is gone," Harold said.

"Grandpa Franklin would probably complain about the statue being made for the front of the Science Department building," Conan chuckled.

"True," Joshua laughed. "He'd want the money going to experiments."

Lark had to do a double take. This was Joshua. Distant, serious Joshua, actually laughing! He had never even cracked a smile in front of her before.

As the evening wore on, she was even more shocked as Joshua remained loose and talkative. She had never seen him this relaxed. She smiled softly, suddenly reminded of Alex. He too was very serious and stern when it came to anything but his family. Hmm. Maybe she had been too harsh in her judgement of Joshua.

Lark slowly opened her eyes the next morning. It felt nice not waking up to an alarm clock. But since there were going to be tons of strangers in the palace for Franklin's memorial service, she had been instructed to stay in her suite of rooms. They were located on the west wing's third floor and included a bedroom with walk-in closet, study, sitting room, small kitchenette, and several rooms that didn't have a specific function.

She sat up on her king-size bed, careful not to disturb Snowy curled up on the pillow beside her. The cat had a cushion in the corner, but they were both happier at night when they slept curled up together.

Very little light peeked through the blackout curtains, but Lark could still see fine. There were perks to having enhanced vision. Still, she had been inside so much the last few days, she missed the sun. Pushing her silk sheets aside, she padded across the thick beige carpet to the window and threw the curtains open.

Sunshine flooded her spacious room, revealing a couple bookshelves, a large vanity dresser, and the doors to her bathroom and closet.

She took a couple minutes to admire the view from her room. Below her was a huge garden filled with sections of herbs, vegetables, vines, bushes, and flowers. Beyond that lay the hospital building she first woke up in. In the near distance, the palace grounds nestled into a heavily wooded mountain.

She'd been impressed while looking over a map of the expansive palace grounds. Whoever designed it knew how to outlast a siege. It was practically a tiny town in and of itself. It could be closed off from the world for years on end and still function fine.

There were people milling about in the garden, but she wasn't worried about being seen. All her windows were tinted so no one could look inside. Apparently, you could adjust the amount of tint, allowing someone a glance inside if you wanted, but she had no intention of changing the windows to her private quarters.

Deciding to continue lounging in her pajamas, Lark grabbed her tablet and went through her bedroom door into the sitting room. All of her rooms but the bedroom connected out into the hallway, but they also had doors in the sides leading to another room. The same generic beige carpet, cream walls, and light purple trim continued through all the rooms, but she had been told she could change whatever and decorate any way she wanted. She was a little busy these days, but that was definitely going to happen when things slowed down. Right now, her rooms felt too much like the maze of hallways outside.

Her sitting room had a large sofa underneath another window looking out over the garden, a dark wood coffee table, and a couple chairs scattered around. She continued on through the study, with its desk, bookshelves, fireplace, and chairs into the kitchenette. There was a small countertop stove that, with a push of a button, you could add walls and a roof to, making it a tiny oven. A small but deep sink took up one corner, and a refrigerator sat next to an empty counter. Cupboards and drawers were full of utensils, place settings, and preserved foods.

After grabbing a bottle of juice from the fridge and a package of cookies from a cupboard, Lark made her way back to the sitting room sofa. She got comfortable and watched Franklin's memorial service. There were lots of dignitaries crowded in the ballroom, only a couple of which Lark remembered from her lessons with Joshua. A small stage was set up on one side of the room, holding ornate bouquets of jewel-like arrangements, and a beautiful, golden urn sat in the middle. Hundreds of chairs faced the stage. The Cynbels sat next to Avi in the front row. Speeches were given honoring Franklin's memory, anecdotes were shared praising his wisdom and genius, and many tears were shed.

Lark stretched and finally went to get dressed as people began slowly filing out. Snowy was still napping on the bed.

Now was the perfect time for her plan.

She opened the hallway door and peeked out. The guard on duty was someone she recognized from the rescue mission, but she couldn't remember her name.

"Is everyone leaving?" Lark asked brightly.

"Yes, your highness." The Spur Corps member nodded.

"Great. I need to run to the classroom real quick." Lark started down the hall.

"But–"

"No one is allowed above the second floor," Lark reassured her. "I'll be quick."

"I could get whatever it is you need," the guard offered, keeping step with her.

"You can't get in the room."

The classroom had biometric locks only Joshua, Harold, Conan, and the royal family were programmed into. At first, Lark thought that seemed a little paranoid, but now it played in her favor.

Her bodyguard wasn't happy, but she didn't object anymore and simply followed Lark up a back staircase to the fourth floor.

"I'll be as quick as I can," Lark said, unlocking the classroom door and slipping inside.

After softly closing the door behind her, she went straight to Joshua's desk. Notebooks and stacks of papers covered the edges of the desk, but those weren't what she was looking for. Quickly glancing through the drawers, she began to worry Joshua hadn't left his tablet here. After a fruitless search, she wanted to punch something. How was she supposed to look at the particle search program if she couldn't get access to it?

She began to root through all the papers, hoping to find any information about time travel. Unfortunately, the parts she could understand seemed to be about history and etiquette. She placed her right hand on the glass desktop and leaned forward to put the handful of papers she currently had back. The desk lit up, and a revolving hologram of the Kynaston family crest hovered in front of her face. Startled, she succeeded in suppressing a yelp, but managed to trip over her own foot as she jerked back. She fell into Joshua's chair and lost her grip on the papers, sending them flying every which way.

I forgot computers are in the desks now. She clutched at her chest for a moment, willing her heartbeat to slow down.

Then an automated voice made her jump. "Password needed to resume program."

"Your highness?" Lark's bodyguard called through the door. "Are you all right?"

"Ah, yes, um–" Lark leaped out of the chair, waving her hands wildly through the hologram–which of course did nothing. "Sorry, I just accidentally hit something."

"Password needed to resume program," said the desk again.

"Hush!" she hissed at the desk. "Off! Shut down!"

To her relief, the hologram disappeared, and the desk went back to being a desk.

Feeling guilty, Lark scowled as she tried to set things back the way they were before she went on her search rampage.

She grabbed a stack of books from her own desk so her bodyguard wouldn't get too suspicious and trudged back to her rooms.

CHAPTER 17

A week later, Lark thought she was beginning to understand Joshua better. His head was so wrapped up in his equations and puzzles that he often came across as cold and unfeeling. He reminded her so much of Alex, it kind of hurt. That single-minded dedication to their interests balanced by a warmness only a few were privileged to experience. The Cynbels all had vastly different interests and strengths, but they were a tight-knit family and deeply respected each other. When Harold and Conan were around, Joshua visibly relaxed. He even smiled, laughed, and joked around.

Joshua had a lot of responsibilities for a twenty-one-year-old. He had inherited Dr. Franklin's positions as head of the Science Department and advisor to the throne. They were renowned across all four planets as unrivaled geniuses.

Evren had four extra months in the year, which meant even though he, Conan, and Shamira were close to her age in number–twenty-three and twenty-one, respectively– they would be closer to thirty on Earth.

Lark got the feeling Joshua had even less experience making friends than she did. But she was really starting to want to count him as one. And even though the nostalgic feeling was nice, she didn't want him as a friend just because he reminded her of her oldest brother. It was awkward when he never seemed to relax around her.

Considering she and Joshua spent all day, every day together, it would be nice to relax out of teacher/student– or even worse–princess/subject personas. She didn't want to feel like a test tube. She wanted to feel safe from herself. She wanted a friend to walk with her through this.

Right now, they were going over the different capabilities of her bracelet, which had been fixed and reinforced so she didn't short it out again.

"You can get a VPhone for personal use, but your bracelet has phone and holographic capabilities," Joshua said.

"Very cool!"

"Put your thumb on the tiger's head, and it will bring up a menu," Joshua instructed.

She eagerly rested her finger on her wrist. After a couple seconds, a black, pixelated box floated above her arm, filled with white words: **Vo-Call, Vid-Call, Text, Maps, Emergency Signal**. She scrolled down. The list went on and on.

"You can have the voice audible for everyone, but there's also a setting where the sound vibrations come only to your ear."

"Ah, is that private mode?" Lark asked, still playing with the bracelet menu.

"Yes," Joshua said. "It will also pick up your voice from the barest whisper."

"Hmm." She started looking for a contacts list to try calling Shamira.

"Oh, I also added my particle program," Joshua said nonchalantly.

She shut down her bracelet to gawk at Joshua. "What?"

"You seemed interested. I thought you would enjoy taking a look at it." Joshua shrugged.

"Yes, thank you!" Lark hoped she didn't look too eager. She had kept her time travel questions to a minimum the last week.

As Joshua began explaining how it worked, there was a knock at the door.

"It's unlocked," Joshua called.

Shamira poked her head in. "Are you guys at a good stopping point? It's almost lunch time, and I promised to braid Lark's hair today."

Lark jumped up before remembering to ask Joshua, "Are we good?"

"Certainly, your highness. Enjoy your lunch. I'll see you this afternoon."

Lark joined Shamira in the hall. Shamira held up a large bag emitting wonderful smells and grinned.

"I've got noodles and cheese with chicken," she said proudly.

"Let's go!" Lark said, dragging Shamira to her room.

ϟϟϟ

Joshua tapped his desk rhythmically, deep in thought. His whole career, he had focused on the science, the puzzles.

Now that he was paying attention to the consequences of his research, he wasn't sure who to trust. Time travel and the bio-bots alone made Lothar a dangerous power. The more Joshua observed King Avi, the more he was convinced he was hiding something. He had his guesses, but nothing concrete yet.

As for the princess, she was smart and eager to learn. Certainly as imperfect a human as the rest of them, but so far, she had the makings of an excellent leader. Now Joshua wanted to know if she would be a queen he was willing to lend his powerful mind to.

He eyed his tablet.

"Okay, princess. What will you do?"

Shamira swallowed her mouthful of food as they sat in Lark's study. "What did this used to be called?" she asked.

"We called this macaroni and cheese." Lark shoveled a huge bite of the cheesy goodness into her mouth.

"Hmm. Now it's called noodles and cheese." Shamira shrugged.

Once they were full, Lark led the way to her bedroom. Her vanity already had a brush, comb, rubber bands, and bobby pins.

"I wasn't exactly sure what we needed." Lark glanced nervously at everything she had set out.

"This is fine," Shamira assured her. "Go ahead and sit. I'll do you first, then you can practice on me."

"Thank you!" Lark flashed her bright smile.

"You have such soft, fine hair," Shamira said as she ran the brush through Lark's dark tresses.

"It's always been thin and straight." She frowned. "I wanted wavy hair growing up. Like yours." She eyed Shamira's relaxed waves with envy.

"There are pros and cons to each." Shamira chuckled.

As Shamira continued to work, Lark's face got happy and serene. Her eyes even started drooping. Shamira grinned to herself. She knew how relaxing it could be to have someone play with your hair.

"How are you so good at this?" Lark asked in a sleepy voice.

"I have younger sisters, all with long hair," Sharmia answered. "Our parents both worked long hours, so I took care of my siblings growing up."

"You do have a very comfortable, big-sis vibe," Lark said, eyes still closed.

Shamira's heart clenched a little. Lark was sweet, and hardly helpless, but did seem a little lost at times. It brought out Shamira's protective instincts.

"All right," she said, tying off the end of the braid. "Here you go."

Shamira chuckled as Lark shook her head, letting the braid fwip around her shoulders.

"Your turn!" Shamira nudged Lark out of the chair and sat down herself.

Lark's eyes got big for a second, but then she looked determined, grabbed a brush, and stationed herself behind Shamira.

"Okay," Lark breathed, brush poised. "How do I do this again?"

Shamira laughed.

"I'm sorry!" Lark chuckled. "I just realized I didn't pay much attention when you did my hair. It was so relaxing, I was practically falling asleep."

Shamira walked her through the beginning steps of a French braid. Once Lark seemed comfortable with the steps, Shamira let herself relax into the rhythm.

"This is fun," she said. "I don't often get my hair played with. I'm always taking care of my younger sisters'."

"Well, this is my first time doing this for anyone." Lark sounded a little embarrassed. "And I'm afraid this first attempt is coming out rather abysmally."

Shamira laughed. "Don't worry about it. The first few are always a little rough."

"I'm glad you're not expecting perfection." Lark made funny faces at her braid attempts. "But I agree, this is pretty fun."

"Did your brothers never do your hair when you were younger?" Shamira asked.

They locked eyes in the mirror before Lark looked away.

"They tried for a bit." Lark smiled. "But it was a lot easier to just throw my hair in a ponytail or bun, so we all got a little lazy. When you were doing my hair, it reminded me of what it felt like when my mom did it." Lark studiously avoided Shamira's eyes, focused instead on what her hands were doing.

"When did you lose her?" Shamira asked softly.

"When I was ten." Lark's voice was tight.

"What about your fa–"

"The same time." Lark's voice was now hard and angry.

Shamira didn't know much about Lark's past, except she had two older, military-affiliated brothers as the family she grew up with. Their parents didn't seem to be a big part of the picture. But if the emotions warring with each other on her face were any indication, it was a lot more complicated than that.

"I'm sorry." Shamira wasn't sure what else to say. Her parents were busy, but at least they were both alive.

Lark seemed to shake off whatever she was thinking about. "Okay, there is no way you can leave with your hair like this!" She held up a rough braid that was already falling apart. "This is embarrassing." She mumbled, undoing her work.

"Don't be embarrassed. You just need practice. Everyone starts as a beginner. We still have time if you want to try again. Otherwise, I'll just pull it back."

"If you're okay with it, I'd like to attempt it one more time today." Lark looked stubborn.

Shamira smiled and handed her the brush.

CHAPTER 18

Lark followed Shamira after hair braiding into the private gym they used to conduct some of the bio-bot tests. The room was huge, with harsh, bright lights in the ceiling. One side was just an open area with thick wrestling mats covering the floor. The other half was filled with gym equipment that Joshua and Raphael had hooked up to their tablets so they could keep an eye on her vitals and data. It always smelled faintly of sweat and cleaning chemicals.

She had arrived in Evren two weeks ago but had only been in Vusal for about a week. They had spent every afternoon exploring her physical skills. The bio-bots had significantly increased her strength, speed, and stamina. Her eyesight was clearer, sharper, and much better at night now. Her hearing was enhanced, but not nearly to the same degree as her strength, so it was easy to tune out most background noise. Her skin would apparently always remain this weird, flexible armor, but it only changed to an opaque black when she was injured or healing.

Lark was looking forward to today, because they were setting boring exercise aside and doing some light sparring to see how her abilities would be used in situations other than running away.

She and Shamira joined the group of people beside the mats. Joshua and Raphael seemed to be comparing something on their tablets. Conan and a couple other Spur Corps members grinned as they approached. They wore slightly bulky, brown, one-piece suits. Cushioned headgear with face masks sat on the ground next to their feet.

"All padded up and ready?" Lark laughed, tapping Conan's suit. There was a thin, hard layer on the surface.

"Ready." Conan nodded and glanced down at their suits. "Josh threw these together. They're supposed to help absorb shock, so you don't have to worry too much about how soft to throw your punches."

"Ooh, good plan," she said.

Raphael came up. "Lark, don't forget these." He stuck little black sensors on her forehead and just beneath her collarbone, then handed her one to put on her stomach. These would feed all of her vitals to Raphael and Joshua's tablets.

After warming up, Lark and a guy with peach-colored hair in a buzz cut circled each other for some light sparring. She kept her chin down, watching Peach Buzz's smooth movements. Forgetting for a moment about her enhanced abilities, she analyzed the situation like she was in a twenty-first century Earth gym.

Her strengths were kicks and elbows. She always tried to avoid being taken down, since she hated groundwork.

Peach Buzz looked strong and had a good build for wrestling. After a couple inquisitive swipes at each other, Peach Buzz attempted a double leg takedown. She jumped back, ending up much farther than she anticipated.

She felt like an idiot.

I can't believe I forgot. I'm stronger and faster now! It still wouldn't do to get lazy, and I should probably ask for help with groundwork, but it will be easier to just muscle my way out of something. Okay! Let's see what I can do.

Making sure to use very little force, Lark ran past Peach Buzz, slicing her elbow across his padded face. She spun back around to realize she had overshot her little sprint and was several yards away from her target. He was still in the midst of turning to face her.

She felt gloriously powerful. Perhaps she had been too stressed during her battle in the woods because it was only now that she really felt superhuman.

Grinning mischievously, she decided to try something fun, fancy, and totally unrealistic in a real fight. She launched forward. Peach Buzz didn't even have time to blink before she leaped into a front flip, bringing her right foot down in an ax kick on his shoulder. She was careful to pull her power before making contact, but Peach Buzz was still sent to his knees.

Lark landed in front of him. "Oh my goodness, are you all right? I thought I kept it light. Did I mess up your shoulder?"

Peach Buzz stood up, moving his head and shoulder every which way, as if to test its mobility. "I think I'm fine."

"Thank goodness," she sighed. "I'm so sorry. I shouldn't have tried that last stunt. I got a little overexcited."

"No, it was actually pretty neat!" Conan said, as the whole group came toward them. "He doesn't get taken down very easily."

"Easy for you to say," Peach Buzz fake grumbled.

Lark could hear the teasing in his voice, but she still winced inwardly.

"Do you have any numbness or tingling down your arm or in your fingers?" Raphael asked, checking his collarbone. "Your data didn't show signs of blacking out, but did you feel close to it?"

Peach Buzz shook his head. "Nothing like that. It's a little sore, but Director Cynbel's suit did its job."

Joshua seemed satisfied. "How do you feel, your highness?"

Lark felt her cheeks heat up. "A little embarrassed, but oddly energized."

Joshua's eyes darkened in thought for a moment before turning to Conan. "Your turn. I want to try something."

Conan glanced at Peach Buzz, but only nodded.

"Princess." Joshua turned to Lark. "I'd like you to try this next part blindfolded."

"What?" everyone gasped.

"You do need to learn what strength parameters to use, but that simply requires time and practice. I also want you to hone your other enhanced skills. You also mentioned you can sense energy. I want to explore that. See if you are 'seeing' electricity, or heat, or something else entirely."

"O-okay." Lark was excited about the possibility, but also nervous about accidentally hurting her friends.

As Joshua tied a cloth around her eyes, he said, "Remember to hold back your strength. This is also training for your control."

"...Right."

At first, the hammering of her own heart thundered over everything else. But as Lark took slow, calming breaths, she started picking out other sounds. A cough here, a rustling there. Now there were spots of color in the blackness. Small, wavering, but alluring. Some shone brighter than others, and most were white with different colored centers. Blues, browns, and reds. One was burnt orange.

"Are you ready?" Joshua's voice came from the area where a group of three dots were.

"I think so," she answered.

"For now, say what you're thinking, feeling, hearing. We'll walk through this together."

Lark was shocked. That was exactly what she had been wishing for all this time. It may have been her imagination, but even his voice had sounded softer, warmer. Not exactly friendly, but supportive.

Maybe we're finally getting somewhere!

"Are you okay?" Joshua sounded impatient. "Do you need a few more moments?"

Okay, maybe not.

"I'm good. Sorry." Lark shook herself mentally. "Who's with you?"

"It's me, Conan," Conan's deep voice said.

"I'm going to have him move around," Joshua said. "See if you can tell where he is."

"Okay."

The dot of light with brown and orange swirls in it started moving to her right. She could hear soft footsteps but concentrated on the light.

"Shall I just face where I hear him? Or do you want me to point in his direction?" Lark asked.

"Whichever you prefer," Joshua said.

Lark decided to do a bit of both. Keeping her body facing the wavering light, she waited until it paused before lifting her hand. "He's there?"

"Very good," Joshua said. His voice was now to her left.

Lark realized with a start that two other dots–one with a dark blue center, one with yellow and green swirls–had joined Joshua's solid white dot. Being so focused on Conan had caused her to miss everything else around her.

There's a lot for me to improve.

Conan's voice cut into her thoughts. "I'm going to move again."

Lark watched his light move back toward the left a few steps. She frowned. She could hear light footsteps, but his dot didn't seem to be moving. The light was growing a little stronger. Before she could work out what was going on, Conan spoke up again, much closer than before.

"Are you okay Lark?" he asked.

Startled, Lark felt a momentary wave of heat through her body, gave a breathless shriek, jumped back, and flung her arms out blindly as a block.

"Whoa!"

"Watch out!"

"Careful!"

"Ahh!"

Multiple voices rang from around the room, followed by the sound of something being hit. Lark tore her blindfold off to see Conan on his back, a tiny trail of smoke floating from a scorch mark on the suit in the middle of his chest. Raphael ran up to him, first aid kit in hand. Everyone soon surrounded him.

"Are you okay? What happened?" Lark asked, a sickening feeling of deja vu coming over her.

"Don't worry, I'm fine," Conan assured her with a shaky smile. "I was just startled. Well, honestly, I was scared witless for a second."

Lark stiffened. "What did I do?"

"Some lightning flew from your hands for a second," Shamira said gently. "It's okay; everything seems fine."

Lark took a step away and hid her hands behind her back when her friend seemed about to come over and comfort her. She wanted to cry, but firmly stamped down the tears. Conan was fine. It was going to be okay.

ʮʮʮ

After assuring himself Conan was perfectly fine, Joshua ran through the data quickly, looking for answers. When he glanced back up, Princess Larkspur had backed up to the wall and was staring at her trembling hands.

"Your highness?" Joshua slowly walked toward her. "Princess Larkspur?" No response. "Princess?" He stopped right in front of her. "Princess Lark!"

She finally looked at him, blinking hard.

"Larkspur." He tried to keep his voice softer. Just because he needed to be firm didn't mean he needed to be harsh. Larkspur's eyes widened slightly, but she was focusing on him. "Conan is fine. He will continue to be fine. We're learning together. You need to acknowledge the inherent dangers and subsequent consequences of what we are doing and not let it freeze you up."

Shamira came up beside him. "We all knew–well, had an idea–of what we were getting into. We signed up for this, Lark."

"But you didn't," Joshua said to Princess Larkspur. Her eyes watered. Shamira and Conan gave him a sharp look, but Joshua ignored them. "You should take the rest of today off and think about what you want to do."

Shamira followed the princess, who barely mumbled something to Conan before fleeing the room.

"Josh–" Conan started.

"Conan," Joshua interrupted, "she is not going to be able to keep everyone safe and happy all the time. As a queen, she will have to make terrible decisions at times. She will be responsible for many lives, and she won't be able to save them all. Her life is only going to get more complicated from here. I don't think that really occurred to her until now."

⚡⚡⚡

Lark didn't exactly run back to her rooms, but it was close. Thankfully, Shamira didn't try to talk on the way, but Lark didn't have the courage to see if there was rejection, pity, or understanding in her eyes when she shut Shamira out in the hallway. Right now, Lark wasn't sure which emotion would hurt more.

She hadn't forgotten that her powers were dangerous, but the last few weeks had been focused on the less deadly aspects of her new life.

She could hurt and kill if the need arose, but that was only ever in protection of another life. If she had lifted her hand a little higher, she could have hit her friend's face with some sort of lightning bolt, or whatever she shot from her hands. At the very least, it could have scarred him for life, if it didn't outright kill him.

She hadn't had people she cared about this much in over two years. She didn't realize she could be this paralyzed by fear of hurting them. Or by the fear of them rejecting her because she was too dangerous. Her head knew that was very unlikely since they were not only great people, but also military personnel who knew the risks they were signing up for. But that didn't stop her heart from freezing with the illogical fear.

Snowy came gliding out from the bedroom, making a beeline for Lark who was still leaning against the sitting room door. Snowy always seemed to know what Lark was feeling.

Scooping the cub up, Lark burrowed her face in Snowy's soft fur.

Why did I even agree to this whole thing?

That question had her standing up straight.

Why did I agree? Stupid Lark! How could you lose sight of the most important thing?

Lark ran into her room, looking for her tablet. She caught sight of it on the bedside table. Snatching it up, she started the particle tracking software Joshua installed.

Time to make some plans!

CHAPTER 19

Lark was pulling her hair back into a messy bun when the clock read 1:30 a.m. She was dressed in a black t-shirt, black cargo pants, and hiking boots. Her trusty backpack waited by the door.

She creeped to the hallway door of her sitting room, held her breath, and strained to hear what was on the other side of the door. She couldn't hear any breathing or heartbeats, which probably meant the guards were still stationed at the end of the hallway. Good. If she was quiet, no one should be any wiser about her exit.

Lark went back to her room, thankful Snowy was still sleeping soundly on the bed. She grabbed her backpack, adjusted it to make sure it was balanced, and then carefully opened her bedroom window. Peeking her head out, Lark searched all around, making sure no one was in sight.

With a deep breath, she climbed over the sill. As she clutched at the ridge with her body hanging slack outside, she took a second to steady her nerves. When she glanced up, she did a double take and nearly let go of the window-sill in shock.

There were two moons in the sky!

Joshua had said something about that, but there had been so many other facts and problems to deal with, Lark had forgotten. Between studies and tests, she was usually exhausted each evening. This was her first time seeing the night sky for several weeks.

Making a mental note to start studying Evren's astronomy, she tried to bring her mind back to the business at hand. But she couldn't help sneaking the occasional peek up as she carefully maneuvered to the side of the window.

Looking down, she inhaled sharply.

When did three stories look so high?

She steeled her nerves, then let go. She let herself fall two and a half floors before kicking herself off from the wall. Adrenaline gave extra strength to the push, and she ended up flying a good fifteen yards from the wall before landing on soft grass. She checked herself, moving all her major joints to make sure nothing was broken. Far from broken, there wasn't even a sprain.

After a quick look around to make sure she was still alone, Lark couldn't help a little giggle.

I can't believe I just did that! I kind of wish I could tell someone.

She tried to get her bearings as she brought the tablet out of her backpack and studied the map. She hadn't had a chance to explore the grounds yet, but she was on the back side of the palace, next to the food garden. If she kept the house to her left, she should hit the orchards, then eventually the stables.

She set off, trying not to look like a suspicious loiterer, but soon gave up on that idea. Attempting to keep the giveaway light of the tablet to a minimum, she only turned it on occasionally to make sure she was going the right way. Lark jogged for several minutes before large shadows loomed ahead, which turned into the orchard behind the east wing.

Finally leaving the palace behind, she quietly made her way to the back of the stables. The murmur of a swiftly flowing river came to her long before the bright moonlight reflected itself in the water running behind the stable. She gave herself a moment to enjoy the serene surroundings before consulting the tablet once more.

"It should be here." She looked around but didn't see anything different. Then again, the particles probably weren't going to be glowing, floating orbs.

She brought her wrist up, placing her thumb on the tiger's head. The holographic menu came up, and she immediately scrolled to an option that had caught her eye when Joshua first showed her the bracelet: **Time Travel.**

Time for some experimenting.

A new list of options popped up when she touched the floating words. After some deliberation, she set the location for right where she was, and the time to three weeks earlier. That way, she wouldn't be crossing her own timeline.

Some stealthy questioning had revealed this area would be free of patrols for the next few hours.

I really hope I did this right.

She cringed a little as she pressed "**Activate**," praying that nothing would blow up. Especially her.

No explosions. Instead, an error message came up on the menu: *Not enough particles at destination to make connection.*

"Now what?" Lark huffed. "How am I supposed to know when there were enough particles?"

Determined to not go back empty-handed, she finally decided to risk crossing her own timeline. But the error message kept coming up for two weeks prior, then one week, then three days. Almost ready to give up, she changed the destination to an hour and a half before her current time. The area should still be clear of patrols.

This time when she selected "**Activate**," she felt a tingling in the air and a soft glow appeared before her, just at the water's edge. She watched in fascination as the muddy liquidesque splotch stretched and flowed, growing until it was a smaller version of the one she had seen on Earth. She waited about thirty seconds, but while the edges ebbed and flowed like before, it didn't grow any larger.

She would just barely fit through this one.

I wonder if I did something wrong? Oh well. I should still be fine. This won't be a very long trip.

After putting the tablet back in her backpack, she debated about bringing everything with her. She wasn't sure what to expect, so maybe it would be good to have the tablet and her emergency supplies on hand. Then again, it was less than two hours in the past, and it wasn't quite the same as last time, so she wasn't sure what would be allowed through the portal.

"Just me this time around."

She set her backpack on the ground, nervously touched her dog tags, and then jumped straight into the portal. A flash of white light, a momentary shock of cold, and she was out the other side...straight into the river.

There wasn't a strong current, but the river was deep in this area, so she found herself completely submerged. Barely resisting the urge to suck in a mouthful of water due to surprise and the cold, she broke the surface and scrambled to the bank. She glared at the portal, still splotched right at the river's edge.

Note to self: Next time, carefully walk through the portal, don't just jump in blindly.

"Did it even work?" Lark searched the area for her backpack.

It turned out to be helpful leaving a marker in the future. After a fruitless search, and noticing the different locations of the two moons, she felt confident she had made a successful trip into the past.

There was a little niggling pain behind her eyes, but nothing too serious or distracting.

Not sure how long portals stayed, she decided to go back. This was enough for the first test. She cautiously stepped through the portal this time, ending up on the riverbank rather than in the water. She smiled smugly to herself as she brought up the menu from her bracelet again and deactivated the portal.

A dark figure stepped from the shadows cast by the stable. "Where did you end up?"

Lark couldn't help a tiny shriek as she jumped backward. She had just enough time to see her hands covered in the blue electric lightning before she crashed into the river. Again.

Joshua watched an impressive display of blue lightning cover the water around Larkspur before it dissipated. He then waited with outstretched hand to help the sputtering princess back onto dry land.

"Maybe we should practice more control over your abilities before another time slip attempt?" Joshua quipped.

She stood in front of him, dripping wet, guilt and embarrassment warring for prominence on her face. "Why...how...?"

"Your highness." Joshua was slightly admonishing. "You're not very good at hiding your intentions. I've known why you wanted to learn about time travel from the beginning."

Larkspur opened her mouth, then snapped it closed again. "Why did you tell me about it, then?" she finally asked.

"Why, indeed?" Joshua mused.

"You don't even know why you're helping me?"

"I wanted to see what you would do. I want to know where my future queen's loyalties lie."

She hesitated. "I wasn't trying to run away, I promise. I just...I want..." She took a deep breath, looked resolute, and stated in a strong voice, "I'm going to save my brothers!"

"What do you plan to do if you can save them? Where will they go?"

Larkspur looked confused. "I thought they would be able to stay with me. Why couldn't they?"

"I don't see why they couldn't," Joshua assured her. "I just thought maybe you were planning on staying in the past with them, or going somewhere else safe, and perhaps less complicated."

She furrowed her brow. "I guess I could've. Why didn't I think of that?"

Joshua actually laughed out loud. The princess sounded as if that wasn't still a legitimate option for her. This is what he wanted to know. Her brothers meant the world to her–of course she would take this golden opportunity to save them. He would do the same for Conan or his father. But now he knew she wasn't about to abandon them here once she got what she wanted.

This was a leader he could be willing to follow.

When he finally stopped laughing and looked at her, Joshua found her staring at him, mouth agape.

"Y-you laughed."

"I'm not incapable of the action." Joshua wondered if he should feel insulted.

"R-right," she stammered. "It's just that, you barely even smile, let alone laugh."

Joshua had to concede that point. "We don't know yet if the past can actually be changed, but I'll do everything in my power to help you save the princes."

"Why?" Larkspur asked suspiciously.

"Because if I were in your shoes, I would do everything in my power to save my family. And I can help you do it as safely as possible."

She tensed. "What about Avi? Are you going to tell him about what I'm doing?"

Joshua hesitated. He now had a choice to make. Where would his own loyalties lie? "No," he finally answered. "I...I'm not sure I trust King Avi fully at the moment."

"What?" Her eyes widened. "What do you mean?"

Joshua felt she deserved to know his suspicions. "I think he's hiding something where you are concerned. I don't know what yet, but I will help you find out."

"You don't trust Avi. Do you trust me?"

"I want to."

Silence stretched between them before Larkspur softly said, "Thank you."

Joshua smiled gently at her. "Of course, your highness."

Her eyes got a little sad.

"Is everything all right?" Joshua asked.

"I want to trust you, too," Larkspur said. "And while, as a princess, I greatly appreciate your skills, I'd really like to have your help as a friend."

Joshua thought for a moment.

He never used to be jealous–all right, not often–of his brother's ability to make friends. He was close with his family, and work brought him all the fun he needed. But having watched Conan, Larkspur, and Shamira grow closer in front of his eyes, he was beginning to feel...lonely. Having a friend sounded...appealing.

Joshua smiled warmly at her. "As a friend, then. Lark."

It was nearly 4:00 in the morning by the time Lark and Josh snuck back to the house. She had decided to call him the nickname Conan and Harold used. So far, he hadn't protested. They now stood three stories below Lark's bedroom window.

The second floor was where King Avi and his late wife had their rooms. And the Cynbels each had a private apartment on the first floor. They of course had family properties across the kingdom, but after Josh and Conan's mother and sister died in an accident nearly seven years ago, the three remaining male members could most often be found at the palace grounds.

"King Avi's rooms face the front, and this is my bedroom." Josh quietly opened the window in front of them. "You should be safe to jump up. Although," he scolded, "you should tell me whenever you plan on going out this way again. There are security cameras and sensors set up along the palace perimeters."

Lark glanced around, her heart beating faster.

"I figured you might try something tonight," Joshua said. "I set the sensors so that they only alerted me and put the cameras on a loop. Once we're back in our rooms, I'll need to set them right again."

She wasn't sure how to feel about her actions being seen through so easily. When she turned to look at him, Josh was yawning.

"Josh, maybe we should start lessons an hour or two later than usual so we can both get some sleep?"

"Good idea. We can make tomorrow a more relaxed day. We can use your study if you think that would be more comfortable."

"I think that would be really nice." She nodded enthusiastically. "Can we talk about time travel and what you're thinking about Avi?"

He seemed to hesitate a moment before agreeing. "That would probably be wise. The sooner we understand what's going on, the better. I'll wait to go in until I know you've made it safely." He looked up toward her room.

"You're sure no one is in that room?" She pointed to the second-floor window.

He nodded. "You can use it, no problem."

"Okay."

Lark backed up a little bit, ran forward, then jumped. She easily caught the second floor's windowsill. Hanging there for a second, she looked down at Josh and gave him a thumbs up. From there, she sprang to her own window, which was still slightly open, and clambered into her room. She poked her head back out and waved to Josh. He disappeared inside, and Lark closed her window.

Snowy had apparently gotten up at some point because the bowl of wet food Lark had left out for her was now empty. But she was now peacefully slumbering again, sprawled in the middle of the bed. Lark quickly got ready for bed, slipped under the covers, and fell into a dreamless sleep.

CHAPTER 20

The next morning, a sleepy Lark, and even more tired-looking Josh, met up in her study. Snowy, having had the best sleep out of all of them, frolicked around the room, chasing the occasional dust mote.

Josh dumped an armload of books, papers, and his tablet onto the desk before they decided to drag the coffee table from the sitting room over to the study's fireplace. Lark brought some energy drinks and glasses of water for them, then settled in one of the soft chairs.

"Let's start with time travel," Josh began. "You did a pretty good job, for a first try. The closer in time and location a trip is set, the more control you have. But you should be careful. There were barely enough particles for you to establish a link."

"Is that why the portal was smaller than the one I originally came through?"

"Yes." He sounded serious. "You should always look for one that stays at least as large as Conan. The edges always fluctuate a bit, but if it stays that large, then you know the connection can last for a couple weeks, if you're not going far away. Location-wise, anyway. We haven't seen an influence on how far away in time you go, as long as there are Wright Particles in the location."

"And they move around, correct? I wasn't able to make a connection to three weeks ago."

Josh nodded. "Correct. How did your head feel during the trip and after?"

She concentrated for a second. "There was little ache behind my eyes during my trip, but nothing much. I don't remember when it disappeared, but it was definitely gone by the time you helped me out of the river." She tried not to blush, remembering her ungraceful fright.

"I'd really like you to try a few more test trips back in your own timeline, but I'm not sure I should recommend it. The bio-bots will probably take care of any damage garnered, but we shouldn't be flippant about it. The main goal is to get the princes, er, your brothers, here safely. Not to see what the bio-bots will heal."

"True."

She needed to be careful. She shouldn't be stupid, thinking the bio-bots would save her from anything. After all, she had managed to nearly kill herself with them.

"So, what do we need to save my brothers?"

"We are going to need a date, time, and location," Joshua said. "It would be best with an exact GPS location, but if we have a rough idea of where to go, we can search for the closest group of Wright Particles."

"Well, I have a date, but we'll have to dig for a time and location," she mused. "I know the day my brothers died, but it was on a classified rescue mission, so I was never told where. And believe me, I searched." She found herself clenching her dog tags and relaxed her grip, willing herself to stay calm. She had to think straight, not get blinded by emotion. Again.

Josh handed her one of his notebooks. "Write down everything you know about that day, and I'll start searching through archives. This could take awhile."

She nodded and began scribbling everything she could remember. Once she was done, Josh sat, poised to take notes himself.

"Now," he said. "Can you tell me more about them?"

"What do you want to know?" Lark asked, not sure where to start.

"Anything and everything," He said. "Hobbies, interests, loves, hates. This could come in handy if their mission fails to bring results. If I have other places to look for them, we can get on their trail."

Always happy to reminisce about Alex and Sterling, Lark launched into story after story.

"Alex is the oldest, ten years older than me. Sterling is eight years older. Alex has–had–blue eyes, while Sterling had these gorgeous gray eyes. The colors my eyes used to be." Lark got a little choked up.

Josh looked uncomfortable, probably remembering the first–and only–time he had commented on her eyes. She had nearly screamed that they weren't her correct eye colors.

"I'm sorry I was so mean about it that first time." Lark grimaced. "It's not like you knew they were going to change my eyes. It's still, admittedly, painful, but I shouldn't have blamed you."

He nodded. "So, what did they do in the army?" he asked a little too quickly.

"Alex was the captain of an Army rescue team, and Sterling was a survival specialist. They weren't always in the same unit, but Sterling had just been transferred over about three months before the...*the* mission. Alex signed up when he turned eighteen, in large part so he could afford college and have a steady paycheck. Our...father... was out of the picture since before I was born. So Alex had been my father figure since he was ten. Sterling and I practically idolized him. In fact, Sterl insisted on joining the army because he wanted to follow in Alex's footsteps. He eventually found out he loved survival training and pursued that."

"What happened to your mother?"

Lark knew he was simply curious, but Josh's question made her tense. "She was killed when I was ten," she answered shortly.

Seeming to realize she wasn't going to talk about that anymore, Josh cut the family history short for today. "Let's talk about your new family."

That only made Lark more irritated. She was a Kynaston now, thanks to Avi. And while it had its perks, she was still sore about being torn from her life and burdened with all this responsibility.

"What do you think Avi is hiding?" she asked.

"I'm not sure yet." He leaned forward. "His insistence on not only you as his heir, but also your adoption had me wondering. Especially your adoption. He could have appointed you heir without that. You are, after all, an adult.

Well, technically you were still a teenager when you first met, but your brothers were undeniably of adult age. I'm not sure if he just wanted to keep the power in his family or if there's another reason."

She mused for a bit. "Honestly, back on Earth, I thought he and Franklin would be cool grandfathers. But now that you mention it, his insistence on me does seem odd. For any of it. I know he wanted a redo for parenthood, but there are plenty of people here on this planet and in this time that he could have used."

He frowned. "King Avi and Grandpa Franklin always treated Conan and me like family. But I have always been attached to Franklin, while Conan was closer with King Avi. He has been, for the most part, a good king. He brought Lothar back to glory after generations of neglectful and idiotic ruling. And I was so caught up in science and experiments, I didn't think about what my leadership was doing. But now, as Director of Science and an advisor, I need to know who, and what, I am supporting."

Lark stayed silent. Josh had obviously struggled with this. She was glad he would be one of her own advisors to the throne. She was even more determined now to be a queen he could look up to and willingly support.

Eventually, Josh looked at the old books he had brought. "King Avi has always been a lover of mythology. But once his wife died, he seemed to become obsessed with it. I wonder if he stumbled upon something in his studies that you resemble."

Her eyes widened. "Me? There's nothing mythical about me."

He gave her a look.

"Right." She remembered the bio-bots. "But there wasn't anything like that when I first met him."

He shrugged. "I brought some of these books about myths, legends, and prophecies on the off chance we might find something. But most likely, you'll need to gain access to the king's private store of documents."

"Me?" she said again, her heart sinking.

"Yes, you." He sounded almost annoyed. "You are his heir; everything will eventually come to you anyway. We just need to help it along. Which means you will need to actually interact with him."

Lark groaned. She usually tried to avoid Avi as much as possible. When she worked with him a few hours a week to start learning the ins and outs of governing a kingdom and when they had their weekly dinner, she used only as much civility as protocol demanded. He obviously wanted more, but she merely treated him as the person she would replace one day. They couldn't stay like this forever, but every time she looked in the mirror, Lark couldn't bring herself to forgive Avi yet.

"Prin–Lark," Josh corrected himself. "He is not all bad. He might have a hidden agenda where you're concerned, but I believe he truly does care deeply for you."

She nodded reluctantly. "We have dinner together tonight. I'll try to ask about exclusive documents."

Now it was Josh's turn to groan. "How about you start by asking about things regarding his interests? Like mythology?"

"Right." She felt sheepish. "That would probably be less obvious."

He shook his head. "I'll try to help you. King Avi asked my family to join you both for dinner."

Lark perked up, hopeful the atmosphere wouldn't be as suffocating with the Cynbels present.

She and Josh each picked a book and started reading. They poured over manuscripts for several hours, with the occasional interruption of Snowy, before a knock at the door interrupted them.

"Come in," Lark yawned.

Shamira opened the door. "It's lunch time. Did you two forget?"

Lark checked the clock. "I guess we did. Do you want to grab something to eat, Josh?" Shamira looked a little surprised at the nickname, but Josh didn't seem to notice.

"Not yet," he said. "I'll try looking into what we talked about earlier." He grabbed the notebook with notes about Alex and Sterling, and his tablet. "You can keep the books here if you want. I'll meet you after lunch," he added before leaving the room.

"Josh?" Shamira asked, after making sure he was too far down the hallway to hear her.

Lark smiled. Today had been more relaxing than she had anticipated. Josh was still Josh, but it seemed he was really willing to be friends. Talking with him was like getting a little bit of Alexander back. Their personalities were similar. The single-minded dedication to their interests, balanced by a warmth only a few were privileged to experience. But soon, she would have both Alex and Sterling. She couldn't wait to introduce them to her new friends.

"Jealous?" Lark teased. "You want a nickname, too?"

Shamira laughed as they left the room together. "Well, I wouldn't oppose one."

CHAPTER 21

Lark ducked the punch coming toward her face. She spun around to catch the sneak kick coming from a second opponent. After getting a better hold of the leg, she sent the owner flying into her first assailant.

Skin buzzing, she jumped back. She took a deep breath, tried to tap into the energy flowing through her body, stretched her hands toward the force field that sprang up around her, and...

Nothing.

"Argh!" She couldn't help stamping her foot in frustration. "I was hoping it would help if my adrenaline was pumping."

Conan shut down the force field around the gym's wrestling mat. Lark had been trying to tap into her stored energy ever since lunch with Shamira. The two sprawled Spur Corps members she had been sparring untangled themselves and sat up.

"Are you okay?" She came over to give them a hand. "I tried to go gently, but I can't always gauge my strength correctly."

"We're fine, your highness," they assured her. "The suits Director Cynbel built helped quite a bit."

Lark studied the matching combat uniforms everyone in the room was wearing. Even Joshua sported the dark brown bodysuit. They were baggy, like a pilot's flight suit, but covered with thin metal plates that acted as a faraday cage. Or they would if she could ever get her body to work with her. They were fire resistant, difficult for a blade to get through, and even slightly shock absorbent. If her strength got away from her, no one had any serious injuries by the time sparring was over. Plenty of bumps and bruises, but no broken bones...so far.

She walked over to the middle of the gym, between the matted area and gym equipment. Josh and Raphael were studying a live hologram of her body vitals. Her body outline was a light green, her blood was more pink than red, and were the white lines her nervous system? It was a little weird watching the pixilated arms move to put hands its on its waist in sync with her.

If she was touching a power source she could manipulate different forms of energy. But she couldn't seem to tap into the bio-bots' stored reserves without that jump start or when she got really startled.

"Your hi–Lark, it's only been a couple weeks since you got the bio-bots." Josh reminded her. "Let's drop this for the moment and focus on the limits of what you can do right now. You still waste a ton of energy every time you manipulate anything. You would be able to last longer and do much more if you learn how to conserve your output."

Lark frowned but nodded.

"Snowy, leave those alone!" Josh snapped at the tiger cub stalking a stack of books near his leg. "Lark, she's awake."

"Sorry." Lark came over to pick Snowy up. "Leave it." Lark carried her over to a playpen set up against the far wall. "We really need to get a covering for this thing. It's way too easy for her to climb out now." She started up an automatic toy to distract the cub.

"Do you want to practice with fire or electricity?" Shamira joined them.

"I'm tired of failing today. Let's play with fire," Lark laughed.

Her elements were fire and electricity. But so far, she had an easier time manipulating small amounts of fire.

A lit candle was brought to the middle of the matted area where Lark sat before Conan set up the force field she insisted on having. Just to be on the safe side.

She held her breath, feeling nervous with everyone watching her every move. She reached her hand out and touched the small flame with her index finger. A slight tickle, then a warm, tingly feeling spread through her hand. Flipping her hand over, she brought half the flame to her palm where the yellow and orange turned to different shades of purple.

"Great," Josh praised. "Now try making it bigger."

When she did this, it almost looked like she was creating more fire out of nothing, which really felt like magic. But Josh ruined the illusion by explaining it was the bio-bots' stored energy that fed it.

Lark concentrated hard, staring at the flickering blaze. Slowly, it grew larger. While she was at it, she formed it into a ball. She hadn't brought herself to admit it out loud yet, but she loved practicing throwing balls of flame because it made her feel like a player in one of the RPG games Sterling loved to play. Thank goodness she didn't have to waste time with a lengthy incantation or kata.

"You're wasting a lot of your stored energy." Josh's eyes were glued to the hologram of her, which now showed an infrared scan of her body.

"Try relaxing your muscles," Raphael piped up. "Don't concentrate so hard. Breathe slow and deep."

"The finesse might be a little rougher at first, but for now it's more important to control the output of energy," Josh added.

She nodded. She rolled her shoulders, loosening her tense frame. As she did, she tried to tune into what her body was feeling. There was the now familiar buzz and tingle all over. A slight warmth everywhere. Hmm. Maybe if she tried to focus everything into her hand? Long, slow breaths. Relax.

"There we go." Josh sounded pleased. "That's getting better."

Lark gave a soft smile, trying to stay laid back. The ball had gone back to a small flame in her palm, but it looked brighter.

"All right, try making different shapes while staying this relaxed." Josh instructed. "This will help your control in manipulating the fire and, later, electricity, to move however you want them to."

She brought it back into a ball of light, then shifted it to a rough pyramid. Sending a long streak of blaze upward and another to the right of her palm, she ended up with a fiery "L" resting in her hand.

Scattered applause stroked her ego.

"You're still wasting energy." Josh's comment brought her back to reality. "But we're certainly making progress."

"Oh, Lark, it's getting near dinnertime." Shamira's reminder brought her high spirits crashing down.

Having lost focus, Lark accidentally absorbed the flames. "Ah, thank you."

"Do you want to walk over together?" Conan asked.

"Sounds good!" She smiled. "I'll take a quick shower and get dressed into something more appropriate. Meet in my sitting room?"

"Your majesty, good evening."

Lark's greeting at dinner felt like an iron gate slamming down on Avi. At least her voice didn't drip with venom anymore. Either she didn't hate him quite as much, or she was getting better at hiding her feelings.

Avi sighed as they all sat around the table. He had brought this on himself. Right now, he was just thankful his appointed heir was actually taking her job seriously. She had a strong work ethic and sense of responsibility. Lark had thrown herself into her studies and already had a decent grasp of their current economic standing. She was making educated decisions and showing wise leadership skills by listening to the advice of those with more experience. He could rest easy if he left his beloved kingdom in her young, capable hands.

The last few rulers before him had been too heavily influenced by growing up with the kingdom's upper class. Between wanting to ingratiate themselves with old childhood chums and being power hungry or lazy, Avi had inherited a country on the brink of ruin. It had taken fifty years of hard work to bring them back to stability and strength. He could trust Lark to continue his legacy. She had a democratic mentality and was more hesitant to abuse her authority as a monarch.

"Thank you for joining us Harold, Conan, Joshua." Avi nodded at everyone. "Shall we eat?"

"I hear training is coming along well," Harold said to Lark.

"Thank you." Lark flashed a grin at Josh and Conan before turning to Harold. "It's been interesting so far. Although the list of things to do and learn seems never-ending."

"I would imagine so," Harold chuckled.

"We need to set an introduction date," Avi said. "We've promised the heir would be coming home soon. Now that Larkspur is finally here, the people really should get to know her as soon as possible."

Lark looked nervous.

"Joshua, when do you think we can have a debut?" Avi asked.

Joshua thought for a moment. "I think she'll be prepared enough within two weeks."

"Two weeks?" Lark yelped. "Are you sure?"

"You don't have to know everything," Avi assured her. "If you've got the basics of etiquette and a grasp of current events, you'll be fine for a debut."

"If you say so." She sounded doubtful.

"You can think of it as a week-long holiday from studying," Harold offered.

Her eyes widened. "A week? This is going to take a whole week? What goes on in a debut?"

"Oh, at least," Avi said. "There's so much to do! First will be a short press conference so the entire country can see you. Then there will be a round of parties and events—" He stopped when he noticed Lark's face paling. "Are you okay?"

She swallowed. "Press? I won't have to make a speech, will I?"

Avi shared a confused look with Harold. "Well, yes. Speeches kind of come with the territory."

"I don't have the best track record when it comes to standing in front of a bunch of people and trying to talk. Or breathe..." Her voice sounded the most faint and frightened Avi had ever heard it.

"Lark?" Conan studied her.

"I'm sorry." Her voice wavered a bit. "I'm just reliving horrible memories of attempts at presenting classroom assignments."

"Don't worry about it for the moment. We'll work on that part together." Avi realized belatedly that wouldn't exactly be soothing for Lark. He frantically looked around for a change of subject. When he locked gazes with Harold, he tried to beg for help with his eyes.

Harold, Conan, and Joshua overlapped each other.

"Um, one of the events will be a martial arts demonstration. That would be interesting, right?"

"We're going to have to start training Snowy if she's to be introduced along with you."

"There will be delicious banquets throughout the week."

Avi dropped his head into his hands. But Lark's laugh had him peeking at her.

"I'm sorry. I'm fine," she assured them. "I just get really nervous and lightheaded when I have to give speeches. Thank you for distracting me."

Avi sighed in relief. "Did you go over dress patterns?"

Lark nodded, color coming back into her face. "At the time, I was told outfits were going to be designed, but I didn't pay close attention to what they were for. After picking out some colors, I told them I trusted their fashion sense better than mine and focused on other things."

"That's understandable." Avi smiled softly. "You've had your plate full. It's tradition for the Kynaston family to wear wisteria purple for their debut. I think it will look very nice with your new, beautiful eye colors."

Avi didn't understand why Conan jumped slightly at that. Joshua tried to give a subtle "No!" gesture. What was wrong?

Avi startled when he looked back at Larkspur. Fury radiated off her, her sapphire and silver eyes glowing. Well, that was new. But why was she so angry?

CHAPTER 22

Lark had actually been enjoying dinner for once. But the idea of a debut spoiled her decent mood.

Still trying to calm her rapidly-beating heart, Avi mentioned her eyes. And she snapped. This was the last straw. She had been trying to stuff her stress and anger down for the last two weeks, trying to accept her new life wholeheartedly.

But this was the one thing she couldn't forgive. Her eyes. She was pretty sure Shamira had said something to the rest of the Spur Corps because no one had mentioned them again.

She had tried hard to remain at least civil to Avi. But now all caution flew to the wind.

"My beautiful new eyes?" she growled. "I hate these eyes." Lark ignored Avi's look of shock. "I *had* beautiful eyes! They matched my brothers'! Alex had eyes the color of a cloudless sky, and Sterling had gorgeous gray eyes. That and their dog tags were all I had left of them!"

She heard sharp intakes of breath from everyone around the table, but her gaze stayed locked on Avi. She knew it was unfair to lay all the blame on him, but he was the main reason her life had changed so drastically.

"I'm so s—" Avi tried.

"I don't want your apologies!" Lark cried. "Give me my brothers' eyes back. I want *me* back!"

Tears caused her vision to blur. She rose from the table without a single goodbye, went back to her suite of rooms where Snowy waited, and sobbed her heart out all over again.

$$\text{ᚼᚼᚼ}$$

Conan knocked on the door of Lark's sitting room. When there was no answer, he glanced at Josh waiting silently behind him. Josh shrugged. Conan rolled his eyes.

So helpful.

He slowly opened the door and poked his head in. "Lark?" He carefully stepped into the sitting room, Josh following close on his heels.

There was no sign of Snowy in the playpen filled with mostly-shredded toys in the middle of the floor. The room's walls were lined with filled bookshelves, but the sofa, window seat, and scattered sets of chairs were empty.

"Lark?" Josh called.

Her voice came through the closed door on their left. "In here."

Lark's bedroom was dark. Flipping on the light, Conan saw Lark huddled on her bed, Snowy frolicking on a mountain of pillows surrounding the girl and her tiger. His heart squeezed at the traces of tears on his princess's cheeks. "May we join you?" he asked quietly.

There was a slight pause before Lark gestured toward the edge of her king-sized bed. Conan and Joshua sat on the foot of the bed, facing Lark. She wouldn't look them in the eye.

"We didn't know they would change your eyes," Joshua said.

Conan glared at him. Was that Josh's idea of an apology?

"I know," Lark sighed. "It's just difficult looking at myself. I'm really starting to love it here. It's fun working with you and the Spur Corps. Sometimes I feel like I'm getting the hang of my new life. And then I see my eyes and feel lost all over again. Like I don't know who I am anymore."

They sat in silence for a little while.

"I don't understand why it has to be me," she finally said. "I mean, either of you would be a much more logical choice for heir than some girl who happened to save him in the past."

"Well, technically Joshua was his heir before King Avi met you," Conan said.

Her eyes got big. "What?"

"The king and queen never had children, and if Casimer gained that power, he would ruin all of the progress we've made as a country," Josh answered. "Conan or I seemed the obvious choices since we knew the ins and outs of the kingdom better than anyone, and their majesties basically took the place of our grandparents. Conan begged to be able to follow in our father's footsteps, so I was named heir when I turned eighteen."

Lark's jaw dropped, which made Conan want to laugh.

"Well, do you want to be the heir again?" She sounded more curious than desperate.

"Are you kidding?" Josh looked at her like she was crazy. "I don't want to rule a kingdom! I don't mind helping you rule one day, as your advisor and Director of Science, but I don't want your throne."

Lark turned to Conan, but he cut her off. "Ever since I was little, my dream was to take over as commander general from Dad. I want to *protect* the king, not *be* the king."

She sighed. "Well, I'd be lying if I said I haven't been enjoying getting an upgrade...in several aspects." She chuckled. "I promised to do my best, and I will. I just... miss certain things about the old me. Probably always will. And I'm already having anxiety about all these parties, speeches, etiquette, and decisions. I mean, what if I do something wrong? If it's not an etiquette thing, I could slip up and reveal I'm from the past. Or, heaven forbid, the bio-bots act up and I suddenly find out I can fly during a national broadcast!"

Conan laughed at that. Josh looked intrigued.

"Look." Conan settled down when Lark punched him on the shoulder. "No one is perfect. Not everyone will like you. And if I'm being honest, I wasn't a huge fan of having a stranger come in to rule. But now I think having some new blood here is a good thing. You might be able to see things with a less biased view. You didn't grow up in a society that prizes the aristocracy, so you won't automatically prioritize them."

She furrowed her brow. "Does King Avi do that?"

Conan shook his head "Not like his predecessors. Grandpa Avi has made his share of mistakes, but he's been a good, benevolent ruler. The people love him because they know he truly cares about them. But when you grew up with a certain group of people, it can be easy to show them favoritism without even realizing it."

"I guess so," Lark said thoughtfully. "You really think I can pull this off?"

"You are smart, capable, and not alone. You can do this," declared Josh.

"I think you will go down in Evren history," Conan added firmly.

She laughed. "What does that even mean?"

Steele's eyes snapped open.

His sparsely furnished bedroom greeted his gaze. He preferred to keep it this way. It reminded him he didn't belong here. This was not home.

He had dreamed about her again. He could never remember much of his dreams, but his last thought was about the girl with the eyes like silver fire and sapphire ice. His head roared in agony, and there was a great aching emptiness on the edge of his consciousness.

There had been an announcement the other day with her picture. She was Crown Princess Larkspur Kynaston-Casimer's replacement. Steele smirked at that thought. There was a press conference happening soon to officially introduce her to the public.

A soft voice cut through his haze of discomfort. "Are you ready?" Beck stood in the doorway.

Beck didn't have problems with migraines like him, but Steele knew he also struggled with nightmares. More than once, Steele had woken him in the middle of the night, only to realize his older brother didn't remember anything that had caused him to toss and turn.

"Yes, all ready. I just woke up from a nap."

Steele followed Beck to meet with Casimer. He was in the middle of a vo-call.

"I will have my best man infiltrating. Yes, I understand you have been very patient. I will remind Steele that time is of the essence. She will help us or–" Casimer angrily threw his VPhone across the room. "I hate that we need them." He crumpled a picture of Princess Larkspur and threw it into the fireplace.

Steele thought it was ridiculous, but Casimer had an entire pile of her portraits printed out so he could do things like throw them in the fire.

"But we do need them," Beck reminded him.

"Yes." Casimer sank dejectedly into his seat. "For now. That little imposter will never have my throne. No matter who I have to partner up with." Catching sight of Steele, he pointed to the table. "There's a copy of the schedule of events for her debut, and the folder has all the documents you need for a new identity. Infiltrate Larkspur's debut."

"Yes, sir," Steele said automatically when Casimer glared at him.

"I don't care how you do it, but either get her here, or get rid of her. If we can't use her, she dies."

Steele lowered his head in a short bow, hoping his face didn't betray his feelings. The very thought of harm coming to the princess filled his heart with dread and guilt. Why guilt?

"I want no more mistakes," Casimer droned, no longer paying attention to him. "We can't afford them. Take whatever you need. You leave in two hours."

Beck clapped him on the back. "Be careful."

Steele nodded to his brother. "I'll do my best. After all, I don't have you watching my six."

Steele walked back to his room, thoughts only partially filled with what persona he was going to take on and which documents he would need. His face hardened with determination. He was going to meet the new princess, but not for the reasons Casimer wanted. He might even be able to turn the tables and enlist her help to rescue Beck.

He quickened his step. There was still a long way to go, but he would get his answers. Or he would die trying.

CHAPTER 23

Over the next two days, Josh watched Lark studiously avoid Avi, and they were thankful he didn't seek her out. But it couldn't last. They eventually ran into each other on the stairway of the west wing. He wasn't sure where King Avi was heading, but they were on their way to Lark's study.

He normally tried to give her free time after dinner, but he had come across something that could be troubling and wanted to talk with her right away. The closer they became, the more comfortable he and Lark were with each other. They had started studying in each other's apartments for a change of scene, and more comfortable furniture than a desk chair. Josh knew he reminded her of her oldest brother, Alex, but it didn't seem like she wanted to replace Alex with Josh. And the more he learned about the eldest prince, the more Josh liked him. He didn't mind being compared to a hardworking, responsible man like Alex.

Avi's copper eyes looked pained when he caught sight of Lark. "Ah, um."

Lark motioned for Joshua and her two escorts on duty, Conan and Shamira, to keep going.

Josh hesitated before following Conan a little ways away.

King Avi had inherited a country on the brink of destruction and had to build Lothar's economic and military stability from the ground up. His goal was to have a peaceful, prospering country where his citizens could thrive, not just survive. While he had obviously made mistakes, no one was perfect. His apology to Lark had seemed sincere, and he was eager to make up for past mistakes. How he would do so was still unclear, but they could get there together.

Except...that little piece of information Josh had stumbled upon today was nagging at him. He stared at the king and Lark as they exchanged words. She had been feeling guilty about her outburst the other day, so she was probably apologizing. And it seemed like she remembered they needed Avi's store of information and was trying to be civil, if not exactly friendly.

Josh was more worried than ever about what the king might be hiding.

"Josh, are you okay?" Conan asked.

Josh hadn't realized he was frowning. Trying to smooth out his face, Josh almost nodded. But realizing he really wasn't, he frowned again. "I'm not sure."

Conan followed his gaze to where Lark and King Avi seemed to be wrapping up their exchange.

"I'm sure they'll be fine."

"That's part of what I'm worried about," Josh mumbled.

"What?" Conan asked.

Josh shook his head. "I've got to talk to Lark first."

Josh finally tore his gaze away from Lark and King Avi and was surprised to see a complicated expression in Conan's eyes. Was he worried? Jealous? Upset that he and Lark had a secret he wasn't part of yet? And if so, was he jealous of her or Josh?

"I'll explain everything when I can," Josh promised. After all, Lark had the right to know first. It didn't seem to satisfy Conan, but Lark came up just then and they resumed their way to her rooms.

She entered first but stopped in the doorway. "Snowy!" Her gasp had them all running into the room.

Josh grimaced, surveying the yards of shredded fabric that used to be the curtains in Lark's study. They were the first personal touch she had made to the rooms, and it was now strewn all over the room. The crimson fabric made it look like a giant had bled all over everything. Curiously, not a thread was out of place on any of the couches or chairs. Today, Snowy had been satisfied with the drapes. Although yesterday, the little cub had chewed and clawed her way through two and a half chair legs in Josh's parlor while they were engrossed in an astronomy lesson. Thank goodness they had noticed her at that point, or he might have had to replace all his furniture.

Today, they had left Snowy in her playpen. A thick blanket fastened on the top had been enough to keep her inside the last few days. But apparently, she had discovered the material was no match for her razor claws.

"We'll get her!" Conan and Shamira scrambled for Snowy.

Lark and Josh watched, amused, after making sure all the doors and windows were closed.

Josh turned to her. "By the way, that cat doesn't get to come into my suite again until she is house-trained. Just imagine if she got into my study."

She cringed. "Agreed."

Nothing top secret was allowed out of the lab. But Joshua, ever the scientist, had turned one of the rooms off his bedroom into a mini lab. It held copious amounts of information. Data he was in the middle of sorting, miscellaneous notes, studies he and Grandpa Franklin had been working on. He shuddered to think of the havoc the frolicsome cub could have wreaked in there. Not to mention the danger of electrocution should she decide the computers, tablets, and projectors made good toys.

"How do you even train a tiger?" Lark asked, watching Snowy lead Conan and Shamira on a merry chase around the room.

Joshua shrugged. "It can't be much different than training a regular dog or cat."

She gaped at him. "For being the smartest person I have ever met, in both worlds–save, perhaps, Doctor Franklin–you can spout the most absurd statements. Have you ever tried training, well, anything?"

He looked at her, brow furrowed. "How hard could it be?"

"A little help?" Conan groused to Lark from where he ended up sprawled on the floor. "She is your tiger, after all."

She grinned mischievously. "You said you'd get her, so I thought I'd give you a chance."

Joshua couldn't help laughing at Conan and Shamira's embarrassed grunts.

"Right, then." Lark jumped toward Snowy with a nearly feline grace.

Joshua hustled out of the way, dragging his brother and Shamira to the empty window seat as he saw a hunter's gleam come into his friend's eyes.

Snowy, still thinking this was a game to play with everyone, pranced around the chaise lounge in front of the empty fireplace. Then she paused to cock her head and study Lark. She must have sensed something, since she stiffened slightly, then crouched, almost mimicking Lark.

Joshua watched, fascinated, as human and tiger stalked each other around the room. He had thought she looked quite graceful and smooth while sparring, or even during mundane activities like running on the treadmill. But playing with Snowy was bringing out a whole new level. It would have been hard for either of them to make much noise moving around on the thick, luxurious carpet covering the floor with how lightly they stepped. Lark was now mimicking Snowy, which was not something they had encountered in their tests and training so far.

Lark slowly herded Snowy toward a corner, the cub's tail twitching in anticipation. Lark's focus was riveted on the tiger, every movement purposeful. And with such grace, she almost seemed to flow from one step to the next. For a moment, Joshua had the uncomfortable thought that his friend had the look and air of an ethereal huntress about her.

Snowy must have decided the same thing, or noticed her ploy, because she suddenly darted forward, attempting to get around Lark to the relative freedom of the open room. Snowy was like a black and white streak of lightning. But she was no match for Lark.

Her arm flashed out so fast, it was merely a blur as she lunged toward her target. She easily scooped up the little cub. Unfortunately, she had used more force in her jump than she realized. Too late to stop the momentum in midair, she gently tucked Snowy into her protective arms, twisted herself so that she landed on her shoulder, and then rolled to her feet.

Straight into a wall.

Lark flinched back from the gouge her head and shoulder had created, but too quickly for her feet to catch up, so she ended up tripping backward and landing on her rump, Snowy still secure and cuddled in her arms.

It was so quick; everything was over almost before it began. Joshua didn't have time to react. He and Lark blinked at each other before he shook himself to jump up with Shamira and hurry after Conan, who was already lunging forward.

"Are you okay?" Joshua asked, staring at the new holes in her wall.

"I'm fine, just embarrassed. Are you okay, Snowy?" Lark inspected the cub before accepting Conan's arm to help her up.

Snowy, still thinking this all a game for her amusement, playfully pawed at Lark's chin and tried to lick her nose.

"Are you in any pain?" Conan checked with more concern than usual.

Joshua narrowed his eyes.

"My head hurt for a second, but it's fine now," Lark assured him. "My arm didn't even change color. Sorry for worrying you. My strength got away from me."

Conan and Shamira checked her over, just to be on the safe side. As they were inspecting her head, Joshua caught a softening of Conan's gaze behind the worry.

Hmm.

"Snowy!" Lark seemed to remember why she had gone after the cub in the first place. "Come with me, young lady."

Conan and Shamira gawked in disbelief as their princess proceeded to pick up the tiger by the scruff of her neck and carry her to the places of destruction she was responsible for. As she scolded Snowy, letting her know in no uncertain terms that she could not destroy property on a whim, Joshua smirked at Conan.

Finished with the lecture, Snowy slunk behind Conan's legs with an injured air. After he kneeled down to stroke her, she sat with a dignified look and proceeded to delicately lick her paws clean.

Larkspur gave a sigh as she glanced around. "I'm going to feel really bad telling King Avi about this."

Conan shrugged, unconcerned about the damage. "This is easily replaced. Nothing of importance was harmed."

She gave a faint smile as Josh raised an eyebrow. That sounded more like something he would say, not Conan. Anything not connected to his family or his research was unimportant to Joshua. He wasn't sure Avi would feel quite the same way. But he had been remarkably patient with the mishaps so far.

"Looks like I still need to work on control." Lark kept that faint smile on her face.

"We can practice together tomorrow after Josh's tests," Conan promised.

Now her face broke into a full grin. "That will be fun."

Josh glanced between the two, still smirking. His older brother was falling for the next queen, although he probably didn't even realize it himself. Which he found hilarious, because of Conan's aversion to the throne.

But really, the more he thought of it, the more Josh liked the idea. They complimented each other well. And when Conan got the next version of bio-bots, they would make the ultimate power couple.

How could he help two of his favorite people along?

"What are you smiling creepily about?" Conan's question broke into his thoughts.

"Just my next project."

CHAPTER 24

Lark thought Josh got very serious as soon as he shooed Conan and Shamira out of the room. She watched him struggle with something as he kneeled to help her pick up all the shredded fabric around the room. Snowy's distraction had eased the tension from earlier and helped Lark forget there were serious matters to discuss.

Not sure if she should try to rush him, Lark waited until they were seated, tablets and notebooks in hand. But when Josh simply continued staring into the cold fireplace, Lark finally cleared her throat.

"Josh, what's the matter?"

He started but refused to meet her eyes. "I don't have much information yet...I don't know what it all means..."

Instead of being annoyed at his stalling, She began to feel scared. It wasn't like Josh to be hesitant in dishing out information.

"You're absolutely sure you gave me the correct data about your brothers' deaths?" he finally asked.

Okay, now I'm getting a little annoyed.

"I couldn't give you an exact location or time, since the mission was classified," she huffed. "But based on the private eye's investigation, I gave you our best guess. And I remember the date precisely."

"That's what I was afraid of," he said, almost under his breath.

She frowned. "What do you mean?"

"In my search for any information we had already gathered on your brothers, I came across the very date you gave me." He hesitated.

"So? You already knew they were killed. It would make sense you had already found out when."

"There was also a time and location. For a time-travel trip."

She still wasn't sure what that meant, but she had a feeling she wouldn't like it. "A trip?"

He nodded. He brought something up on his tablet and shoved it at her. "There were lots of trips made in our search for you all. But apparently, a small Wysteria Unit made a trip on that day to Earth."

"Why?" Lark was beginning to feel queasy. "Any why didn't you remember it?"

"I wasn't involved." He shook his head. "It looks like Grandpa Franklin was the one in charge of setting it up. It was about two years ago, our time. I wasn't even on the planet. There was a huge Technology and Science conference on Atlantis I was attending. It was the first year I went without Grandpa Franklin."

"Then what was the trip for?" She was really feeling sick. Was it possible Avi or Franklin were involved in...no. That was a crazy thought. This was all crazy!

"I'm not sure yet. That's all I found so far, but I thought you should know. Lark!" Josh pointed to her face, looking worried. "Your eyes are glowing again!"

She closed her eyes, trying to calm down. There was no telling what she might accidentally do if she didn't stay in control. She gripped the arms of her chair.

"Wait, Lark—"

But it was too late. The delicate scrolled wood splintered in her hands. "I didn't mean to do that."

"You should probably let off some steam," Josh said. He looked anxious, but also like he was trying not to laugh.

"But we need to find out–"

"We will," he promised. "But right now, I need to make sure you don't burn down the city."

"That's a little harsh," she mumbled. But she still followed him out into the hallway where Conan and Shamira were chatting.

"Lark!" Shamira's smile froze when she caught sight of Lark's face.

Conan jumped forward. "What's wrong?"

Lark looked at Josh, not sure what to do.

"Not here." Josh glanced around, then motioned for everyone to follow him.

Their group silently made their way through the night to the orchards behind the palace. Josh still refused to say anything as he followed the river behind the orchards upstream. Lark did find herself relaxing as they walked swiftly for more than fifteen minutes. The ground was a smooth carpet of dark green grass. The moons were only partly hidden by clouds tonight, so the occasional wild-flower caught their light, flashing like jewels.

The river, which was shrinking more into a stream, led them into a forest. Lark's guards had been keeping an eye on her the whole trip, but she was thankful they hadn't asked any more questions.

Josh eventually stopped next to a small pond covered with lily pads. "How are you feeling?" he asked Lark.

"Better, thank you."

"Now can you tell us what is going on that you had to bring us somewhere no one would hear us? I've half a mind to call dad."

"Don't!" Josh surprised all of them with his vehemence.

"What is going on?" Conan asked again, now sounding suspicious.

Josh looked at Lark, waiting for permission. This was, after all, mostly about her.

Lark bit her lip, not sure what to say. These people were her friends, but they had been Avi's subjects for far longer. Could she trust them? She played with her dog tags. If she was going to figure out what was going on and save her brothers, she would need more allies than just Josh.

She took a deep breath. "I think Avi might be hiding something. Josh and I are conducting...an investigation. One I don't want Avi finding out about." She stood tall, looking Conan and Shamira straight in the eyes. Who would they choose?

Conan was visibly struggling internally, but Shamira stepped forward.

"I chose to follow you to my dying breath the day you insisted on going back to save the hostages." Shamira kneeled on one knee, which Lark found a little excessive.

"Um, thank you." Embarrassed, Lark helped her back up. "I appreciate the sentiment, but you really don't have to kneel." She looked at Conan. "I know I'm asking a difficult thing from you. I completely understand if you don't feel comfortable. I only ask, if you decide not to help, to leave now and forget tonight ever happened." She tried not to sound threatening, but she wasn't sure she entirely pulled it off.

Conan looked like he was close to walking away. But he just looked back and forth between Lark and Josh. "Are you sure this is warranted? It's to be expected Grandpa Avi wouldn't share everything with you right away. I mean, he has the responsibility of most of this planet resting on his shoulders."

"It's a little bigger than that," Josh said quietly.

Conan stared at him for what seemed an eternity. But Josh's seriousness seemed to be what tipped the balance. "I'm with you, Lark," Conan finally said. "But I also believe if you find your suspicions baseless that you will make it up to Grandpa Avi."

Lark nodded. It couldn't be easy suspecting someone you look up to and love so much. She figured Conan was still loyal to Avi, but at least he was willing to listen to them for now.

"If we're wrong, I will personally tell Avi everything and apologize," she promised.

Shamira looked at Josh. "What is it that has you so worried?"

Joshua motioned them all over to where he'd plopped down on the grassy bank next to the pond. Everyone gathered around him.

"There's a possibility people from our time may have been involved in the princes' deaths."

Lark heard soft gasps, but she didn't look at anyone. She kept her gaze out over the pond. Josh quickly went over what Lark and he had found out...which wasn't much.

"Wait, did you say two years ago?" Conan's voice sounded tight. "Can I see the data you have?"

"I haven't gone through it all," Josh said, but still handed his tablet over to his brother.

Conan began to read, the tablet's glow throwing exaggerated shadows across his face.

"Okay, a team was sent on the day the princes died," Shamira said. "But Earth is a big place. They could have gone anywhere."

"This is the timeframe in which we know they died," Josh countered. "And if that wasn't enough of a coincidence, the location fits with the approximate area Lark was able to find in the past."

"That doesn't prove—" Shamira began to protest.

But a strangled cry from Conan had everyone looking at him.

Lark didn't think the harsh light from the tablet was the only thing making his face that pale.

"What's wrong?" they all chorused.

"Dad was part of that mission," Conan choked out.

Lark's heart sank.

"That's not unexpected." Josh frowned. "He headed about half the time missions."

Conan shook his head. "You don't understand. Dad was nearly killed during a time mission two years ago."

"You guys said it was nothing!" Josh accused. "'Just a little limp,' you said."

"By the time you got back from your conference, it *was* nothing," Conan mumbled. "But it was pretty bad at first."

"How could you not tell me?" Josh hissed.

Lark and Shamira tried to pretend they weren't there.

"What could you do from Atlantis?" Conan hissed back. "He stabilized and began to heal right away. Dad didn't want you to worry."

Josh glared at his brother.

Lark felt for Josh, but they really needed to move on. "What does this mean?" she asked Conan, but he seemed to be in shock.

Josh, now pointedly ignoring Conan, was the one who finally answered. "It's not looking good for King Avi, Grandpa Franklin, or my dad."

"Yeah, but why?" Shamira asked impatiently.

"Because," Conan said in a voice devoid of emotion, "it's entirely possible this little jaunt brought Casimer to the princes."

"Wait, Casimer is involved? How?" asked Lark.

"Casimer had a spy in our science department," Josh reluctantly admitted. "Before we found out, he had gotten his hands on technology that let him piggyback on some of our time travel trips. It seems he followed and attacked the Wysteria Unit in the past. If they were anywhere near the princes' team..."

"It was our fault?" Shamira whispered.

Now they were all in shock.

Lark felt sick to her stomach. Unlike Avi, she really liked Harold. She was even thinking about asking if she could call him uncle.

But if they were actually responsible for Alex and Sterling's deaths, or even *knew* about it, could she forgive that? Would they have ever told her? Or did Avi still hope to have a loving relationship, forever keeping their secret in the dark?

Lark locked eyes with Conan. He looked like his entire world had been ripped away from him. She opened her mouth to comfort him, but nothing came out. She knew what it was like to feel betrayed. After all, her own father... but at least she had never loved, respected, or idolized him.

Conan struggled to his feet, as if a great burden weighed him down.

"Conan?" Josh jumped up.

Without responding, Conan stumbled back the way they had come.

"I'll go with him." Josh looked worried. "We've got some things to talk about. Shamira, would you see Lark back?" Barely waiting for their acknowledgement, Josh took off after Conan.

As she followed Shamira home in somber silence, Lark wondered when she had started crying.

CHAPTER 25

The next week was a dizzying blur for Lark.

She, Josh, Conan, and Shamira were almost always together. If they weren't in lessons, they were training. If not training, they were attempting to get Snowy to obey commands. And every spare minute they had, they were huddled together researching or pooling their knowledge. They hadn't managed to figure out why Avi chose Lark in the first place, but it was now clear the Wysteria Unit that traveled to Earth the day Alex and Sterling died were ambushed by a heavily armed group led by Casimer.

The Wysteria Unit wasn't prepared for a full-on battle, just a reconnaissance trip. They took heavy damages and had to retreat home. Not many details were in the after-action report, but it did state there was a group of Earth natives that got caught in the crossfire. No survivors.

When Lark read that, she nearly fried the tablet by accident.

There still wasn't concrete evidence Alex and Sterling were there, but Lark was having a hard time *not* assuming Avi, and even Harold, was responsible.

It made their meetings awkward, but Josh reminded her they would get nowhere by shutting them out completely. Ironically, Avi and Harold seemed pleased their little group was growing so close.

If they only knew it was at their expense.

But right now, all that was pushed to the back of Lark's mind. She was in the middle of the dreaded press conference. Due to her constantly voiced fear of fainting in front of the cameras, a table and chairs were set up on the stage, where Lark and Avi currently sat side by side.

The audience was packed in–some with tablets, a couple with notebooks. Cameras were now palm-sized half-orbs, and instead of a long lens, there was a small hole. It then scanned whatever it was pointed toward and sent a live feed straight to projected or hologram televisions.

The only relief to the whitewashed walls was the huge, colored Kynaston family crest hanging behind them.

When Lark had appeared with Snowy in her arms, there had been a huge buzz in the room. They hadn't acted scared, which she thought would have made sense; because hey, there was a tiger cub in the room! They didn't even seem overwhelmed by her cuteness, which Lark found weird; because hey, there was a tiger cub in the room! They seemed more in awe of both Snowy and Lark.

The tiger did make for a great opening topic, helping the press conference start smoothly.

Snowy had grown nearly a foot in the last couple of weeks, beginning to outgrow Lark's shoulders. Sadly though, she was still too small to block Lark from all the curious eyes boring into her.

"How does it feel being adopted by the most powerful king on our planet?" a reporter called from the back of the room.

Here it is. I have to decide.

She could feel Avi tense beside her. She was sure the Cynbels and Shamira were doing the same. She hadn't actually said out loud she would accept the adoption. Technically, if she renounced the royal family, that might be grounds for taking Snowy away. Lark dared anyone to try. But in the end, she chose the smoothest path for her brothers. If–*when*–the rescue was successful, their future would be set if they were part of the most beloved and influential family of the country.

A new life, a new beginning. I am now Larkspur Bei Kynaston.

Lark took a deep breath, trying to settle the tornado of butterflies having a kung fu tournament in her stomach.

Don't faint!

"It was...a bit of a shock when I heard I was chosen as heir." She hoped her smile wasn't too tense. "I am excited to be here," she said truthfully. "And I hope to build upon the Kynaston legacy."

Avi sighed with relief so softly that only Lark could hear it.

"We were all sorry to hear about the princes," someone yelled, shoving their camera and mic forward to catch everything. "Do you wish they were here?" This joker was obviously just trying to get a dramatic reaction. Apparently, that hadn't changed in two thousand years.

The tension in the room grew thick. Questions about her brothers weren't supposed to be asked today. She figured this reporter would be canned. Perhaps even the entire news outlet they worked for. Wysteria Corps members were already surging forward to escort him out. But since they were broadcasting live, she couldn't just ignore it.

It might actually be a good opportunity to lay some groundwork for her brothers' arrival.

"The *disappearance* of my brothers haunts me every day." Lark stared straight at the troublesome reporter, who couldn't seem to keep eye contact. "But since their bodies were never recovered, I still hope to find them one day."

A buzz filled the room. Lark caught sight of Josh against the back wall, frantically motioning for them to stop. Shamira, next to him, pointed to her eyes.

Oh no. Are my eyes glowing again?

She just had time to see Josh and Shamira head toward the door before Harold stepped in front of their table.

"No more questions," he said. "You will have your chance to speak with the royal family again in the coming weeks."

Harold and Conan escorted Avi and Lark out the back door.

Avi turned to Lark when they were away from the prying eyes of the press. "Lark, are you wanting to try to rescue Alex and Sterling?"

Her eyes flashed at him, but he wasn't sure with what emotion. "Is there some reason I shouldn't try?"

Perhaps accusatory?

"I'm not sure the past can be changed," Avi said warily. "Or what the consequences would be if it can."

Not to mention the prophecy...

"What good are all my powers and this technology at my fingertips if I can't use them for the most important people in the world to me?" she asked.

"I don't want you to get hurt if we can't save them," Avi said softly. He hoped upon hope Lark would believe the truth in that statement, but she still looked skeptical. "All right," Avi sighed, realizing she would probably do it behind his back anyway. It wasn't just guilt that prompted his decision.

Maybe the warning won't come to pass if I help.

"Lark!" Shamira and Josh called as they ran down the hallway toward them.

"Your majesty." Shamira gave Avi a respectful bow.

"Shamira." Avi acknowledged her with a nod. "You are joining the celebratory dinner tonight, right?"

Shamira grinned. "I wouldn't miss it, your majesty."

"Good." Realizing the friends wanted to talk together, Avi motioned for Harold and the accompanying Wysteria Corps members to walk ahead with him. "We'll see you at the private dining room in a bit then. Well done, my dear, on a successful introduction to society."

⚡⚡⚡

"I thought we were keeping the rescue mission a secret!" Josh hissed at Lark.

"I'm sorry." Lark felt like hitting her head against the wall. "At the time, it seemed like a good idea so their appearance wouldn't be so sudden."

"Well, it was quite the press conference." Conan didn't sound entertained.

"Who knows how many people are going to try to weasel their way in here as your brothers?" Josh complained.

Lark winced. She hadn't thought about that.

"At least your eyes didn't glow too much." Shamira tried to cheer her up. "Josh saw it early enough to alert the commander general. And hey, you didn't faint!"

"True." Lark laughed. "Thank you, Josh."

He just grumbled.

"Come on, I'm hungry!" Conan herded them down the hallway. "Dinner is waiting."

"I don't have a working prototype yet," Albert Renat admitted to Casimer. "But I think I'm close," he added quickly.

"Close is not good enough!" Casimer glared at his chief scientist. "I've already lost Franklin. The only thing our allies agreed as a replacement for him was *working* time travel. I don't deliver time travel, I don't get an army. Figure it out!"

Albert's glassy eyes dimmed as he rubbed his temples. "It's getting difficult to concentrate. I just need a little more time."

"You're running out of it," Casimer snarled.

This fool was becoming less useful by the day! When Albert first came from the capital, he perfected the camouflage cloak and learned how to piggyback on time travel trips through a stolen Wysteria bracelet. But with each passing month, Albert seemed to be getting stupider. Well, maybe more confused than stupid. He was always moaning about his aching head. Four years later, and he still couldn't instigate time travel!

"Figure it out," Casimer ordered, "before I figure out how to replace you."

CHAPTER 26

The following days were a rapid succession of parties and events held all over the city. Most were hosted by other prominent citizens, giving Lark a chance to mingle with the most influential members of her new kingdom.

Now she stood nervously behind the large, closed double doors of the palace's ballroom, waiting to be announced for the final occasion of the week. The boring cream walls and purple trim actually felt familiar and comforting at the moment. The festivities were being wrapped up with a large banquet held in the palace's public dining hall and ballroom.

"Are you okay?" Shamira asked with a chuckle.

"Just nervous." Lark tried to still the wobble in her smile. "Snowy, leave my shoes alone."

Snowy kept running around, testing the length of the leash she clipped onto. Lark was hoping the purple harness would prove enough of a restraint on the cat's contortionist skills.

"You've done great this week. This is the last of it for a while," Conan promised.

Lark tried to distract herself by admiring how her friends looked in their formal uniforms. Matching black, fitted suits allowed for ease of movement. Cords of wisteria purple draped off the shoulders and matched the tux stripe running down the side of their pant legs. Shamira had a couple of small medals on her left chest. Conan had a few more, and they both had the Spur Corps crest on their shoulder straps. The silver bracelets and a shiny belt holding a laser gun completed the ensemble.

"You guys clean up well," Lark said teasingly. "Very nice."

"Well, thank you," Shamira laughed, giving a small twirl.

"You look every inch a queen." Conan said warmly.

Lark felt her face heat up a bit. She wasn't used to compliments on her looks, and for some reason, one coming from Conan made little flutters join in the dance of nerves in her stomach.

"Thank you," she mumbled.

She smoothed imaginary wrinkles from her skirt. She had to admit, the light purple formal dress suited her much better than she originally thought it would. The material was light and airy. The floor-length gown didn't poof, but it also wasn't skintight. It hinted at rather than hugged her curves. She originally thought the sweeping sleeves would look ridiculous, but she quite enjoyed the regal feel of them. A fashionable black belt wrapped around her hips and met in front with a silver buckle in the form of the Kynaston Crest, which matched the necklace resting just above her collarbone. She hated heels, so was thankful for the strappy silver sandals.

Surprising herself, Lark had instantly fallen in love with the small tiara nestled in her fancy half-updo. Thin silver branches interlocked and twisted, ending in a point at the top. Tiny jewels shone throughout the design.

She heard footsteps coming before Avi and Harold rounded a corner.

"I'm not used to dressing up," she admitted. "I think I've worn more makeup this last week than my entire life."

"Well, it suits you, dear," Avi said as he approached.

Avi and Harold looked absolutely resplendent. Harold's suit was close to Conan's in design, just forest green instead of black. And, of course, his chest was full of medals. Avi wore a black tux, complete with tails. His cummerbund and tie were wisteria purple. He wore the Kynaston crest as a medallion around his neck.

"Thank you." Lark gave a deep curtsy. "You look amazing."

Avi beamed at her.

She hadn't been avoiding him as much this last week, and he seemed to take that as an overture of friendship. He didn't seem to consider she *couldn't* avoid him because of all the events. But she had been making a conscious effort to speak with him more. She was still guarded, but she was curious how much he would actually help where her brothers were concerned. And how much he would still try to hide.

Now that she had officially accepted the Kynaston mantle, she wasn't sure how to classify Avi. He was more than just the king she had to learn from, but definitely not a trusted friend, either. Maybe she would never be able to see him as true family. Which made sharing a name with him a little awkward. But for now, she had to act at least polite while in the public eye.

Avi held his arm out. "Are you ready?"

"I sure hope so." Lark's stomach knotted a bit more as she scooped up Snowy.

"You have been exemplary." Avi patted the hand she had wrapped around the crook of his elbow. "I am very proud of you."

She didn't respond because the double doors in front of them opened. A loud voice proclaimed, "His Majesty, King Avi Kynaston. Her Highness, Larkspur Kynaston, crown princess of Lothar."

Larkspur Bei *Kynaston*.

She let Avi lead her onto a balcony overlooking the lavishly decorated ballroom and smiled at the applauding citizens.

Don't faint, don't faint, don't faint. Why hasn't this gotten any easier?

Her eyes roamed the edges of the room and picked out the reassuring Wysteria Corps clad in forest green and the black uniforms of her Spur Corps, which helped her light-headedness. She tried to pay attention to Avi's speech, but she kept getting distracted by the hair colors. They were nearly as varied as the clothes. She wasn't used to purple, green, and blue being natural.

Just as she caught sight of Josh, Snowy grabbed everyone's attention by leaping from Lark's arm onto her shoulder.

"Snowy!" Lark hissed.

But the cub, undisturbed, merely wrapped herself around Lark's neck and yawned.

Flushed with embarrassment, Lark peeked at Avi apologetically. But he was beaming at her. Risking a glance down, everyone seemed to think it was absolutely adorable.

"Well, I shan't keep you any longer from the festivities. Enjoy!" Avi smiled at the people below.

She carefully followed him down a grand staircase to start mingling with the guests. She was immensely thankful for the comforting presence of Conan and Shamira behind her and sighed with relief when she saw Josh waiting for her at the bottom.

Conan and Shamira were her bodyguards tonight, so Josh had offered to be her escort for the evening. She had eagerly accepted, relieved to have a friend nearby who didn't have to be on alert for danger.

She had every intention of going around the room, greeting people on her subtle way to the delicious look-ing spread of finger foods and deserts. But she barely moved ten feet from the stairs before she and Josh were surrounded by people. Some of them she had met over the last week, others used their acquaintance with Josh to be introduced to Lark.

As the evening wore on, the constant stream of people were all blending into an unending chorus of ingratiating flattery and probing questions, with the occasional hunger pain.

Josh smirked as he caught her for the seventh time looking longingly toward the food.

"I had them keep some food aside in our rooms in case we don't eat here," he assured her.

"Thank you!"

Eventually, Lark had Shamira take a frolicking Snowy back to her rooms, wondering how much longer they had to stay. She was so tired, and it was past midnight. The crowd finally started thinning around 2:00 a.m., and Avi said it would be perfectly acceptable to leave the party.

After saying her thanks and goodbyes, Lark led Joshua, Conan, and Shamira out of the banquet hall.

"Let's cut across the throne room," Conan suggested. "That'll be the quickest way to the west wing."

⚡⚡⚡

Steele had been watching Lark all evening. Throughout the week, he had many opportunities to get close to the princess, but they had all failed. Every time he saw her, his head started splitting. The last time he attempted to approach her, his chest felt like it was ripping apart. Tonight was his last chance. It would be much more difficult to infiltrate the palace after this banquet.

Would he even be able to reach her at this point? It could all be for nothing, but he would have to take the chance. The risk was worth it. He might lose his life trying to get some answers, but it was better than living like this. Perhaps if he gave himself time to slowly approach her.

Sometime in the wee morning hours, he left the banquet hall to retrieve his cloak. But instead of leaving, he entered the bathroom, put it on, and activated the camouflage function.

He shimmered for a moment, then disappeared into thin air. Moving slowly to not interrupt the camouflage, he skulked on the edge of the banquet hall. He was shaking and could barely stand by the time Princess Lark left with three other people.

Steele carefully followed them into the opulent throne room, his condition worsening with every step. His plan had been to follow them until Lark was alone and then reveal himself. But he wasn't sure he'd last that long. Nausea threatened to overcome him any second. His legs not only shook, but also felt like lead shoes were attached to them.

He made sure to stay at least three yards away from them and not make any noise, but Lark kept looking over her shoulder, frowning, and shaking her head.

"I'm so glad this week is over!" Her joyful voice caused his head to feel like it was shattering.

He stumbled.

Lark turned and looked intently in his direction. Steele couldn't check to make sure his cloak was still working, but he assumed it was since Commander Cynbel whirled around, alert but confused.

"What's wrong?" Conan asked.

"I thought I was just tired," Lark said, "but I keep sensing someone nearby. And I could have sworn I heard something just now." She closed her eyes and shook her head back and forth. "There's a light somewhere over there." Eyes still closed, she pointed right at him.

"Get her out of here!" Conan commanded.

Steele's blurry vision saw Lark being herded out of the room by Director Cynbel and a woman with hair the color of fire.

No!

He didn't think he could survive much more of this. If she disappeared now, he'd never get answers. He threw off his cloak before falling to the floor.

"You!" exclaimed Conan. Steele felt lucky he didn't shoot him out of shock.

"What's going on?" Lark's voice sounded somewhere in the distance, making Steele's head ring.

He soon found himself surrounded by uniformed guards. "I need to see the princess," he gasped, struggling to his knees.

Conan's voice was cold as ice. "You can't."

"You don't underst–" Steele's voice disappeared as his strength slipped away.

The floor was getting closer...oh. He had fallen down again. The cool tile felt good. Was this the end? After all his struggle, he couldn't even talk to Larkspur? Larkspur. Why did that name send a warm spark into his chest?

He felt himself slipping away.

"Wait!" Larkspur's scream echoed and bounced around the walls, stunning everyone into silence.

Steele's eyes back open. When had they closed?

"I know him!" Larkspur's eyes kept everyone at bay as she ran toward him. They had turned darkly danger-ous, glowing with an inhuman light from within. Steele's fevered brain thought he could see actual sparks coming from them.

But they melted with affection as she gathered Steele into her arms.

"I know him," she repeated softly, a world of meaning no one in the room could begin to understand in her voice. Her words reverberated inside Steele until he could no longer think straight. He clutched at the girl desperately. His vision swam and his body convulsed. He felt that he would lose consciousness at any moment, but he knew this girl.

He had to protect her. Take care of her. He was responsible for her in the absence... absence of what?

"...ling?"

Steele knew his senses were being overloaded. He didn't know what would happen to him if he continued to struggle. But he could not give up even if his head exploded. He had been lied to. Something precious had been ripped away from him, even though he couldn't remember what.

He strove with all his might to fight off the dizzying waves of darkness.

He had lost his sense of sight and now he couldn't feel his fingers, though he was sure they were still clinging to poor Larkspur with an iron grip. Like a lifeline. Even with his valiant struggle, his consciousness still steadily faded away. Sweet oblivion looked so welcoming compared to the pain of his mind being torn apart.

Somehow, he knew that if he lost here, he would never come back. Just as he was losing his resolve to battle on, Casimer's annoying face and voice came to mind. Steele couldn't process what he was saying, but he was sure from the tone that it had something to do with Casimer's belief that Steele belonged to him.

As much as Steele hated Casimer, the memory of him was exactly what he needed at that moment.

I refuse to die listening to your voice!

His rage resurged, sending a new wave of pain. But carried on the wave, a different voice cut through the fog.

"Sterling! Sterling, can you hear me?"

He still felt like he was being torn apart at the seams, but Steele swam toward that voice. Though it brought unbearable pain, he knew that voice was his salvation.

Ignoring Casimer's cold, demeaning tone and pushing aside his sulky figure, Steele clawed his way toward reality and Larkspur. He called on the last of his strength to blink his heavy eyelids open. His gaze focused on jewel-like eyes and the unending tears pouring out of them tugged at his heart.

Here she was. His key. Steele's key to the mystery haunting his life like a shadow.

He smiled to himself right before the last reserves of his strength snapped, and all was a sweet, painless darkness.

CHAPTER 27

Lark silently commanded herself to fight the urge to shake and scream at the body she cradled. When he had started convulsing, Lark instinctively held onto him. When another dozen or so Spur Corps members surged into the room, she glared at them.

"No! Don't touch him!" she screamed, hunching her body around the man she was now certain she had once known as Sterling. His eyes had been unfocused, crazed, but those beautiful gray orbs belonged to her second brother.

The protective ring of guards took a step back. She had never been so desperate in her life. Conan yelled for Raphael. The air seemed to crackle with electricity. Sterling's strong body had started to calm down. He still struggled internally with something, but he had settled with his head in her lap, arms locked around her arm.

Lark's friends buzzed around them nervously, but she ignored them and kept talking to Sterling, leaning over his face. "Sterling, can you hear me?"

His tired eyes finally opened long enough for him to give her a small smile, then he relapsed into unconsciousness.

At first, she was afraid he was dead, but she could feel a weak pulse. She looked up, bewildered, at Raphael cautiously approaching. When had he come in? She watched his movements like a hawk, willing him to understand she would protect this man with her life.

"What happened?" she asked.

"I'm not sure," Raphael said. "I need to look at him, princess."

"Be careful." She finally let her medic examine Sterling.

Raphael waved a small stick over Sterling's body, getting a scan of his vitals. "I've got to get him to the hospital." Raphael looked to Avi and Harold for permission.

Lark finally took a look around her. Wow. When had all these people come in?

Raphael called in more doctors on their way to the hospital. She heard him say something about not understanding the brain waves. Feeling shaky, she stayed with Sterling as he was quickly set up in the private room that she had first woken up in. Nurses and doctors came and went, taking scans, administering IVs, and making solemn faces.

She stayed in the corner, refusing to let Sterling out of her sight.

One of the doctors stopped in his tracks, eyes darting back and forth from Steele's comatose state to one of his screens. "Hypno?" he said out loud, his tone incredulous.

That got everyone's attention.

"Hypno? Steele is a Hypno?" The whisper buzzed around the hallway outside his room, filled with Wysteria and Spur Corps members.

Lark turned to the smartest man she knew, Joshua. "What is a Hypno? What is going on?"

She didn't want to interrupt the doctor, who had blocked everyone out and gone back to his machines. Josh, Conan, Harold, and Avi huddled with her in the corner. Shamira peeked in through the open door.

Josh hesitated, giving Sterling a long look. "How do you think you know Steele, princess?"

As impatient as she was to have everything explained, Lark knew he only called her "princess" in private when things got serious.

"His name is not Steele; it's Sterling. He's my brother." Lark looked at the shock on everyone's faces. She understood the feeling.

"Are you sure?" Avi asked.

Not trusting her voice, she nodded.

"And you're sure this is the Steele who held you when you retrieved Lark?" Avi asked Harold.

He and Conan also nodded.

But as Lark studied the faces of her companions, she noticed a gleam of newfound respect toward Sterling. This didn't make any sense. How could Sterling be here, what was "Hypno," and why did being one change everyone's attitude?

She grew impatient and noticed her skin buzzing with her nerves.

Calm down. The last thing we need is for you to burst into flames.

"What is Hypno?" she asked again.

"It's kind of an urban legend," Joshua finally explained. "Lots of people have heard about it, but few actually know what it entails. Hypno is short for Hypno-Slave. It's something of a cross between hypnosis and brainwashing. It's been outlawed due to the extreme danger, not to mention the breach of human privacy rights. You literally toy with the person's brain. Manipulating memories, even rewriting them. It's so taxing on the brain and body that most people die after any attempt. They are the lucky ones. A few survive, only to live out the rest of their days in torment. Half of their brain cells are in constant flux. They're never sure if they're in reality, reliving a memory, or experiencing something someone else put in their head."

Lark shuddered, looking at the man she was sure she had called brother in what felt like a past life. A past life for both of them, apparently. She was reminded how fragile life was as she compared the pale, broken form in front of her to the laughing, boisterous second brother of her memories.

"And then," Joshua continued, "there are people like Steele. The rare few who are strong enough to somehow survive 'Conditioning.' At that point, whoever has done the Hypno process has complete control over them. They are loyal to the point of dying and will do anything they are told. The hitch is that they need to have some sort of contact with their 'Sponsor' within a every day or two, or the conditioning unravels, and madness takes over. Even then, they tend to die within six months. The strain is just too much. If we're correct, Steele is fighting an unimaginable tax on his mind and body. I've never heard of someone being able to war against the Hypno effects. Steele is a man of legend to survive all this."

"Sterling," she whispered, gazing at his prone body for a long time, tearing up.

What had Casimer Talbot put Sterling through? She vowed to find out and do whatever it took to bring her brother back.

Muffled voices cut through the surrounding blackness. Can't see anything. Can't understand anything. Who's talking? Straining, the voices started to become clear.

"...I'm her oldest brother. It's my job to worry about her. And I know she took excellent care of herself and Mom while we were on deployment, but she's been through too much for a girl her age. She should just be a happy, carefree, high school girl. I want her to at least have nothing to worry about when I'm around."

Silent blackness.

"Sterling! Can you hear me? Please, please come back to me. Snowy! Those wires are not for you to play with!"

"Sterl! You're up early! I haven't got the picnic food ready yet."

The oppressive blackness gave way to disjointed images. Wooden...cabinets? Hand-drawn pictures stuck on a white door.

"That's all right." Steele yawned. *"I only just got up. Let me get a drink, then I'll help you finish."*

"Aw, thanks. And morning!"

Hazy pictures solidified into a messy kitchen. A young, dark-haired girl stood on a step stool, reaching into a cupboard. Stomach grumbling, Steele turned to the refrigerator, messy colored-pencil drawings taking a place of prominence on the door. Short arms encircled him from behind as he tried to open it.

"Morning, Larkie." He paused as a cold, wet sensation imprinted itself on his stomach and back. *"Larkspur! Yuck. What are you getting all over me?"* He twirled around, holding her at arms-length to scrutinize the young girl.

"Oops." She grinned at him sheepishly. *"I forgot. The blender decided to be ornery today as I was making a smoothie. It got all over the place."*

Her blue and gray eyes sparkled. They made him dizzy. His vision kept fading and then coming back.

"Including you, I see." Steele rolled his eyes.

"I know how to get that cleaned up right away." The young girl gave a wolfish smile.

Larkspur. Steele–no, Sterling. He was Sterling–can't quite remember how he knew this girl. Or why he felt so responsible for her happiness and safety.

"Oh really?" Sterling watched himself drop his arms from Lark.

"No, wait!" he struggled to bring his arms back around her. "Don't let go! You can't lose her!" But try as he might, Sterling couldn't get them to move an inch.

"Yep." Lark grabbed the extendable faucet from the kitchen sink and pointed it right at him.

Sterling's eyes grew wide as he realized what was about to happen. *"Wait, Lark, no!"*

But it was too late. Lark sprayed his entire body with icy water.

Finally escaping the barrage, he wiped his eyes to see Lark clambering into Alexander's arms.

"Figures," Sterling muttered.

Relief surprisingly washed through him. Why would he feel like such a burden was lifting at the mere sight of Lark with Alexander? *"You need to get cleaned up, Lark, then you can wake Mom."* Alexander started carrying her upstairs.

Lark laughed. *"I'll get stronger and bigger, then I can protect you both, too!"* she called down the stairs.

Sterling smiled to himself. He wished Lark could stay nine forever. But whatever happened, whoever came in and out of their lives, there would always be the four of them.

The world faded once more into darkness

"Look, we've been researching as much as possible for the last two days, but Hypno-Slave technology is not our area of expertise," Raphael said apologetically. "There's just too much we don't know. It was an illegal secret that didn't get far beyond the experimental stage before being discovered over a hundred years ago."

"I can see why," Larkspur muttered grouchily.

She had barely moved an inch from Sterling's side unless it was absolutely necessary. She felt constantly on the verge of tears, which was irritating. It was driving her crazy to be stuck doing hours of research with no results except more headaches.

"It's strange," Josh said from the chair he had appropriated in the corner. "I've spent every spare minute looking into our records. There isn't a lot there. But instead of hypnosis, this process almost sounds mystical–not scientific."

"Maybe we should look into myths and legends?" she suggested. "They often came from a grain of truth."

They already had a bunch of material for their other project. They would just add Hypno-Slave to the research list.

Josh's eyes narrowed as he probably thought about where to start. Her friends had decided to keep a rotating watch with her. She was grateful for their comforting presence.

Why hadn't she studied psychology? Or mythology? Trauma medicine had been her goal, but ironically it wasn't coming in handy now. Sterling's brain had been traumatized, not so much his body.

She had been promised a few days of vacation after the packed debut week. But she hadn't imagined spending them watching over her supposedly dead brother's unconscious body. Sometimes he would moan, sometimes thrash about blindly. But more often than not, he just...lied there. Cold and silent. Fighting an internal battle that she couldn't hope to understand or help.

"Sterling..." Lark's voice broke. She sank into her usual chair next to his bed, bowing her head over his limp hand.

"How are you feeling?" Josh asked. "Do we need to head to the lab?"

When her skin got buzzy, she worried about accidentally shorting all the machines in the room. So she would occasionally head out to burn off some extra energy.

"I'm fine. Just a little tired. And hungry."

"You try to get a nap," Joshua urged. "I'll go make you some food so it's ready when you wake up."

"Just some leftovers or a sandwich is fine," she hedged gently.

Joshua narrowed his eyes. "That wouldn't be you trying to say something about my cooking skills, would it?

Because I don't want to hear it from someone with your track record."

Lark snorted, trying to cover a laugh. Back on Earth, she had pretty much lived off takeout, macaroni and cheese, and instant noodles. For an unrivaled genius, Josh was almost as bad a cook as herself.

"We should take a cooking class together," he suggested.

"That sounds fun!" She smiled. "I've always wanted to learn how to make crème brûlée."

"How about let's learn how to make an edible bowl of soup first?" Joshua looked amused.

"Very well," she lamented. "Soup before complicated desserts. Sterling wouldn't be able to eat much else for a while, anyway. I should probably learn to make something that won't kill him."

"He'd probably appreciate that." Joshua sighed with resignation.

Everyone had long since stopped reminding Larkspur there was a good possibility Sterling would never wake up again. And if he did, his mind could be mush. From the little bit they had gleaned from their research, the Hypno-Slave process sounded like horribly cruel torture.

Lark lost herself to memories when Joshua left.

They started out nice, with fond early moments exploring with Alex and Sterling, their mother teaching her how to read. Mapping out stars with her brothers. But inevitably, the harder memories came in. Her mother cruelly murdered before her eyes. Losing the only other family she had left.

After miraculously finding one of her precious loved ones, she wasn't sure she could handle losing him again. She immediately squashed any hope about Alex.

When they asked how Sterling had ended up here, the obvious conclusion was that Casimer had brought him. Whether he knew who they were was uncertain, but it seemed logical to think Alex had been brought to the future as well. But if that were so, did he suffer the same fate as Sterling? Did he survive the ambush on Earth? Was he–

Wait until we know how Sterling survived. Don't get ahead of yourself.

"Please," she murmured, head lowering to the bed as she drifted into an exhausted sleep. "Please don't leave me again, Sterling."

Before her brain could register to wipe away the tear rolling down her cheek, merciful sleep swept away the heart-wrenching memories and fears.

CHAPTER 28

In between the dreams, Sterling slowly pieced himself back together. Memories of who he was and what Casimer had made him into started to separate themselves. His identity was revealing itself to him, although not always in chronological order, making things harder to keep straight.

Every now and then, a pleading voice would draw him, but reaching for it brought too much pain, and he was still missing too much. But now, the voice he knew belonged to the girl with those mesmerizing eyes, was crying. It was filled with so much anguish, he couldn't ignore it.

He could remember little of anything, and make sense of even less, but one thing he knew–he was responsible for the girl, Larkspur. His whole being was devoted to her protection. After his failure long ago, he had made a promise.

He couldn't recall how, but he had lost her. He had lost himself. But here was a second chance. He would not waste it. He was supposed to have been her solid foundation. But instead, she had found him and brought him back to his sanity. Whatever they had been to each other before, he owed her his life. And he would spend the rest of it trying to repay her.

Sterling became conscious of pressure on his hand.

Taking a moment before attempting to open his eyes, he tried to reign in his overloaded senses. He was lying on a comfortable bed with soft sheets covering him. He could hear the soft whirring of machines nearby. A strong smell of disinfectants.

After a short battle to lift his eyelids, he had to blink away the tears that sprang forth from the assault of light on his pupils that had remained covered for...he couldn't even guess how long. He hoped Lark was near since he was burning with questions. But the first thing his tired eyes focused on was the startled gaze of an unfamiliar young man.

Wait. He looked familiar. Tall, muscular, with short, dark blond hair and blue eyes wide with shock. Before he could figure out why he knew this man, there was a slight shift in the pressure on his hand, causing both males to turn toward the sleeping Lark.

Sterling's breath caught.

Here she was! His anchor, finally within reach. Now if he could just move his hand. Concentrating all his energy on the action, he reached gaunt fingers to brush a strand of hair from her cheek. He and the blond man glanced at each other before their attention was again diverted to Larkspur, who was stirring awake.

"Mmm...is it time..." Lark's sentence hung in midair as she and Sterling locked onto each other. Time seemed frozen as a thousand questions and emotions passed unspoken between them.

Unfortunately, the monumental effort of bringing himself into focus had taken its toll. Try as he might, he couldn't keep Lark's face from blurring.

"No, no, Sterling, stay with me!"

Sterling felt terrible about it, but he simply could not stay awake any longer.

I'll be back. Just wait for me, was his last thought before slipping into a delicious sleep that was actually restful.

He couldn't remember ever feeling this tranquil and whole.

ϟϟϟ

"No, no, no, no, no!" Lark wailed.

Conan lunged forward and grabbed her before she could shake poor Steele. No, Sterling. "He needs rest, Lark! Think!"

"But he was awake!" She staggered back into his arms. "And all I could do was look stupidly at him. I didn't even say hello! I've imagined this moment over and over, and that was not it!"

Conan liked the feel of her in his arms, but he pushed her away so he could look her in the eye. "Larkspur!" He was worried. Lark didn't often completely panic. She blinked rapidly a few times before her eyes finally focused on him. "What's done is done. We can't change that. There's no use lamenting it. Pull yourself together. Us blubbering around will not help him at all. First off, we need to call the doc."

"Right!" She brightened. "He woke up, Conan! He woke up!" She gripped his arms so tightly, he winced. "Vid-call or vo-call? Oh, who cares?"

Then she was off like a shot pulling out her VPhone.

He heard her voice fade down the hallway before he could point out the uselessness of her meeting the doctor along the way. It wouldn't get anyone here faster. But he figured she was too excited to sit still.

Conan stayed by the bed. He had been so surprised to see Sterling's gray eyes open. Too shocked to move. They were not the eyes he had been expecting–the eyes of a mad man yearning for peace. Instead they held questions, but also hope. His gaze was so full when focused on Lark. Full of love, of memories. So different from the look he threw at Conan afterward.

That look had burned. Sterling was defiant, protective, challenging.

What surprised Conan even more were his own feelings about this man waking up. The friend in him should be thrilled that Lark's brother had survived something as horrible as Hypno-Slaving. But Sterling posed a problem. How had he been near their landing point with a small army last month? Was any of the Hypno-Slave still in effect? What other threats were they not aware of yet?

Lark came barreling back into the room, Raphael and Josh in tow. She impatiently watched the doctor check Sterling's condition.

"At the moment, all I can say is he seems stable, even if he is unconscious again." Raphael didn't give anything away behind his poker face. "I have to go study the data from the last half hour."

"May I join you?" Josh asked. "I'm curious about the brain wave scans."

Raphael nodded. "Certainly."

"But he seems to be okay for the moment, right?" Lark asked.

"As far as I can tell," Raphael said rather noncommittally. "And before you ask, no, I do not know when he will wake up again," he added as he left the room.

"I'm very happy for you." Joshua gave Lark a quick hug before following the doctor.

"This is a good sign, right, Conan?"

"I guess we'll find out."

Thankfully, Lark didn't seem to notice his conflicting emotions.

"You'll come back to me," she said, resuming her watchful position with more energy than he had seen in her for a long time. "You remember me," she added happily. "I saw it in your eyes. Yes, you'll come back to me."

"He remembered her. I saw it in his eyes!" Conan insisted. "I don't know why or how, but that man's mind is working just fine."

He and Josh were updating Avi and their father in the king's office.

"I'm not sure if this is good or bad," Harold admitted. "Of course, I'm excited it's possible to survive something like Hypno-Slaving, but what do we do with him?"

Avi frowned thoughtfully. "You're right. We don't know if he's completely free of the Hypno-Slaving. But he is officially my son," he added in an imperious tone. "He will be given due respect, and we will do everything in our power to make sure he can live prosperously here."

"Have you been able to ascertain where his cloak came from?" Harold asked Josh.

"It seems to be an improved version of the prototype we came up with several years ago," Josh said. "We temporarily put it aside to focus on the bio-bots. We hadn't even gotten the camouflage to work yet."

"Someone obviously did," Conan pointed out.

"Yes," Josh mused. "I don't know who yet, unfortunately. But they did a brilliant job. Once the cloak covers you, it will even erase your heat signature!"

"If Sterling can actually remember things correctly, he could be an invaluable resource," Harold said. "Aside from knowing who is capable of inventing this type of device, we need to know how our technology is being stolen. We'll also start an investigation to see how far the leak goes."

Conan listened quietly to everyone debate the pros and cons of Steele–Sterling–making a miraculous recovery. "I don't think Sterling will ever listen to anyone other than Lark," he finally interjected.

Avi and his father turned inquisitive gazes at him.

"Think about it," Josh piped up. "He's like Lark. A man out of time. And if he can remember everything that happened to him, well...if I were him, I wouldn't trust any of us."

"Perhaps he will eventually, once he sees Larkspur trusts us," Avi suggested after a pause.

"Are you sure she does?" Conan asked quietly.

No one broke the tense silence that followed.

Sterling heard soft voices. Opening his eyes was much easier this time. He was still on a comfortable bed. The large room felt a little crowded with a group of four young adults chatting. Two men, two women.

His gaze zeroed in on a familiar profile.

"Little Larkie?" Everyone jumped at his hoarse voice. It was disconcerting to be stared at by three strangers and your baby sister. "What happened to your eyes?" Sterling furrowed his brow.

Tears filled those jewel-like eyes as she came forward to hold his hand. Her skin felt weird. Not scaly, but hard?

"Are you Larkspur?" he asked. Her face looked like it, but some things were not adding up.

"Yes!" she sobbed. "It's me, Sterling. I can't believe we're talking right now." She beamed at him.

Ah. Yes, that was Lark's smile.

"How are you feeling?" She stroked his cheek. "Do you need anything? Water? Food? Wait, can he have food?" She turned toward the silent group.

"I'm not sure," the tall, lean blond said. "Shamira, will you call the doctor?"

The red-haired woman disappeared from view.

Sterling looked at Larkspur again. "What happened to you?"

"That's...a little difficult..."

"There will be plenty of time for that." The red-haired woman rejoined the men at the foot of his bed.

"Who are you?" Sterling asked coldly.

"Oh, sorry." Lark smacked her forehead lightly. "These are my friends–Shamira, Conan and Joshua." She motioned to the redhead, the familiar muscular blond, and then the lean blond.

Sterling gave a small smile, but stayed silent.

Joshua nodded at him. "We should give you two a moment."

"Thank you," Lark called as they left the room.

Seconds stretched into a minute as brother and sister stared silently at each other. A yawning emptiness grew between them.

"What do you remember?" she finally said.

He searched his memories. "I'm not exactly sure what's true and what isn't."

Lark nodded. "Then I'll tell you what I remember. A lot has happened. But basically, I lost you and Alex two years ago. You were on an Army mission–"

"A rescue mission!" he said. Fuzzy, disjointed memories seemed to organize themselves in his mind. "Al's team got tagged for a rescue mission."

Their oldest brother had joined the Army at eighteen. Sixteen-year-old Sterling and eight-year-old Lark absolutely idolized Alexander. Despite Alex saying he should do something else, Sterling insisted on following in his footsteps two years later. Sterling was thrilled to eventually be assigned as a survival specialist for Alex's rescue unit.

On the day in question, Al's team needed an extra member, and Sterling volunteered.

"All I could find out was that your team got ambushed at some point," Lark continued. "Your bodies were never found."

He shook his head. "I can't remember any of that."

"That's all right," she said quietly. "Don't strain yourself. You've been through a lot."

He nodded, but there was something tugging at the edges of his brain. He felt like he was missing something important. He closed his eyes, thinking.

After volunteering for the mission, what was the next thing he remembered?

Pain, needles, distorted images. Casimer Talbot. Beck Jones.

His gray eyes flew open.

"Lark!" He clutched at her. "Alex is alive!"

ᔕᔕᔕ

Lark's breath caught in her throat. She felt dizzy. Was that relief? Hope?

"Y-you're sure?" her voice was breathy.

"Yes, but Lark," Sterling winced in pain, "something... something happened to us. I don't know–"

Lark's eyes widened. "Is Alex a Hypno, too?"

He wrinkled his nose in confusion. "What's a Hypno?"

"Uh, it's complicated. And honestly, I don't completely understand. Some sort of hypnosis, possibly combined with magic? Basically, your heads were messed with."

"Yes!" He relaxed back onto his bed. "Our heads..."

"Who did this to you?" Lark felt fury burning inside her.

"Casimer Talbot," he said with angry conviction.

She nodded. "That's what we thought, but I wanted to be sure I hunted down the right person."

"You know him?" He looked surprised.

"Yeah, well, we haven't technically met. But I'm pretty sure he hates me."

"Oh, he does," he agreed immediately.

That didn't make her feel any better.

"He hates the princess with a passion. Wait." Sterling grimaced, holding his head. "Princess? Casimer? You're... oh, I'm so confused."

Join the club

"Hang on, careful!" Lark pulled his arms back down. "You've still got IVs in."

"We need to save him, Larkie!" Sterling looked haunted.

Her heart squeezed. She turned toward the door. Voices and footsteps were coming down the hallway.

"Of course we're going to save him." Lark's voice hardened. "But you rest now. We need you to heal and remember."

There was a knock.

She turned toward the door. "Come in."

Wait for us, Alexander. We're coming for you!

THE END